# Empty the Sun

# Empty the Sun

A Novel by
## Joseph Mattson

Music by
## Six Organs of Admittance

℮

A Barnacle Book, Los Angeles

◆◆◆

Distributed by Drag City, Chicago

Trade Paperback Original Printing, First Edition.
Published by A Barnacle Book, Los Angeles.
Distributed by Drag City, Chicago.

Artwork by Becky Smith.
Book Design by Tamra Rolf.

ISBN-13: 9780982505625
Library of Congress Cataloging-in-Publication Data is available upon request.

Printed in Canada on 100% postconsumer recycled paper.

A Barnacle Book & Record
PO Box 46232
West Hollywood, CA 90046
contact@abarnaclebook.com
www.abarnaclebook.com
www.emptythesun.com

*RJS*

And for the women, for the music, for the whiskey—
indeed, friends, there are a certain Heaven and Hell I know
within and without because we've gone there together—
a holiest of trinities, amen.

*Ay, in the catalogue ye go for men,*
*As hounds and greyhounds, mongrels, spaniels, curs,*
*Sloughs, waterrugs, and demiwolves are clept*
*All by the name of dogs.*

—William Shakespeare, *Macbeth*

*And if I thought she didn't love me*
*I'd take morphine and die*

—Nehemiah Curtis 'Skip' James, "Drunken Spree"

# ONE

# Chapter One

HERE I was, doing ninety on the Santa Monica Freeway with a quart of whiskey shoved into my crotch and my dead neighbor in the trunk. It had come time to leave Los Angeles. I'd had a dream the night before, *the* dream: God told me to shove a sawed-off slug barrel shotgun into my mouth and pull the trigger—*Why not?*—for the world was going to end in a week, on July 4th. I'd gone to tell Hal, my neighbor, about it—he had a critical obsession with both guns and the Lord—when I found him slunk into his favorite chair like wet clothing stripped after a heavy rain, already stinking of mold and turning blue. He had a pen clutched in his right hand and a piece of paper lying at his feet with the salutation "Dear Magg," shakily scrawled across the top.

Jamming into the iron face of heavy fog sailing inland from the ocean, I couldn't see fifteen feet in front of me, but I could still see Los Angeles in the rearview mirror. The glowing towers of the heart of the bitch gleamed through the hard black of night, and I thought, Soon this fog will cloak you, you poor shameless woman you poor city plagued with hunger you poor insatiable Our Lady, the Queen of the Angels, and I'll be gone. You took him, and though I am not surprised, I still cannot believe it. Hal wasn't just a neighbor. He was a friend. He'd paid his dues.

Belief has always been for noble fools. I conceded: I uncorked the whiskey and shoved the barrel of *that* into my face. It was June 28th. I had six days.

I went west as I always seem to do when leaving a place behind. The problem was that one can only go west for twenty miles from downtown Los Angeles to the continent's end, and no boat awaited me there. I didn't have a plan. I just knew it was time to go. I couldn't bear to let Hal rot away into anonymous oblivion in The Amigo, the ramshackle hotel we lived in which decades before had been a toy factory warehouse. If dreams were once born in the belly of that old building's former incarnation then they sure as hell went back there now to die. No, too many unsigned bodies had been hauled out of that place already. Disaffected former wives surrendered to alcohol, abused and saintly prostitutes, zombie junkies with no discipline, general head cases fried too long under the unforgiving Southern California sun, vets, the discomfited scarred and obese, unknown Blues legends, and a score of forsaken others. The Amigo was first-rate for the crestfallen. Refuge is not a pretty thing. Hal and I ended up there for a similar core reason dressed up in different circumstances: We were each wholly alone in the world after losing something we couldn't afford to lose, which opened a hole so deep in our lives that absolutely nothing could possibly fill it.

Hal had spoken to me about Maggie just once by name, but every single part of his existence was inspired by and reeked of her.

"Real love is the one thing that might give credence to the existence of any of our Gods," he'd say, treading the thinnest line between cold brutal torment and hot ecstatic joy. "Beyond any other cruel or beautiful thing of nature!" Hal had lost his many years ago on a crusty old farm in southwestern Michigan in an incident, he contended, that betrayed—and spilled—the warmest of blood. Hal was the first person I ever met who had killed somebody.

"Forget the universe, fuck the stars, and to hell with the ocean and the miracle of conception. Screw the mountains, too. They all have nothing to do with God, boy. You understand? You listening?"

He was in his sixties and looked not a day younger than eighty yet somehow remained strong, weathered to what I once believed was the point of indestructibility; resigned with boundless sorrow, sure, but unable to die. Until yesterday—presently, literally, a lifetime ago. Beliefs get shattered and then the fools contemplate, so it goes. Yeah, I listened to Hal. He was charming enough. As for understanding, I've my own ideas about God.

I laid the thumb and three fingers of my left hand on the steering wheel as if studying a splayed taxidermied game bird nailed to a board. The index finger was missing. The absence of it glowed in the dim warmth of the dashboard light like an old ghost, dead but soulful, a distant echo of the living. I found the whiskey again and plugged it hard, wiping my mouth with the back of my good hand, missing trickles of wet gold tributaries running through my three-year beard. I reached down between my legs for the mouth of the bottle. Into it I rubbed the fingerless nub of my left hand, brought it to my lips, sucked down to the knuckle, and asked aloud, "Finger, you waiting for me in heaven?" I half expected the ghost to reply, "Heaven, no. Otherwise." What I got was the sound of the air screaming through the slight crack of the window.

All I ever wanted to do in the world was play the guitar, which was execrably ruined when I'd lost the most crucial digit used in my craft just before Hal came into my life and I moved in next door to him. If by chance God was only choking my leash about Armageddon, I'd merely turn a bruised, ripened Christological thirty-three years old in a few months, come Virgo season, and I somehow felt older and younger, dead and alive in the same breath. Yet who am I to say what it's like to feel the thus far untread paths, older and dead? The testament to such things was stiffening into a J-shaped carcass wrapped in an old woolen blanket and curled around a spare tire amid countless emptied quarts of motor oil in the trunk. Hal was also the first dead person I'd ever touched.

Yet in that moment I did not fear the body. No, for the first time in my life what I feared was leaving. Leaving Los Angeles. Gone would be the long bleached avenues of warm disquiet, the whispering seven-story palms towering with wise endurance above the mashed commutes of countless human insects stitching paths across each others' sordid lives, nestled below the caustic trademark layer of smog that governs the puppet show, where hope and despair collide in intersections of the same blue smoke that aspirations are made of and then burned to. And with it all, the sanctimony of place. I feared losing the city with neither indifference nor nostalgia. I'd simply gotten too used to it. In its familiarity lived my fear. Los Angeles is tough and scary and undeniably superb. Nothing if not polarized, the city is mean yet forgiving, dirty yet lovely, full of darkness in its harsh burning light, full of light in its cool darkness, all laid bare without apology or expectation. Almost human. Assholes are assholes unabashed, angels are angels undefined. It is the most honest place I have ever known. And for better or worse, it had become my place. I had come to know her in all of her rotten shortcomings and her rotten promise, in all of her despicable ugliness and numinous beauty, and simply in knowing her I was afraid to leave. I feared even leaving the smog and the tired lungs it'd given me. In the right kind of light, at 7 p.m. in the spring, 8 in the summer, 6 in the fall, 5 in winter—at twilight's turning—as the sun lets the hills go and moves on to cast its belted fist upon the sea, the smog refracts the most brilliant mix of orange and purple, a sight both overwhelmingly apocalyptic and hopeful. The color had come to define what I was now afraid to admit I was leaving: home.

It was the same color that broke through the tattered blinds of Hal's window in occult shafts as I rolled him up in my mother's old wool blanket, the same light that followed me out to the car as I heaved the burden an hour before leaving. The blanket is embroidered with a giant wolf's head and three geese chasing the sun. It was given to me years ago, in a time long before I had lost the finger and other things, and the jolting image of the beast's barren jowls wrapped around the ass of my main man, my patriot, as he lay face down legs bent backward as kneeling in prayer, in execution, before I slammed the lid against his calcifying backside, was all too much.

I bore down on the gas, ignoring the unsure rattling of the engine and the sporadic, nervous flashes from the beams of other travelers slicing breakneck through the fog, openly apologizing to Hal every time I heard his body bounce up with a dull thud against the trunk if I failed to miss the jarring potholes or scanty asphalt fillers lining the four lanes of road like open wounds and petrified scabs. I gargled down more whiskey with the spirit of piss and blood, bitter but necessary. The smell of bile creeping up.

Ten more minutes into the fog and she was gone. The lights and the distance obscured by the mist, the mirror filled with nothing but wafts of gray and black, and I still didn't know where I was going. I rolled the window fully down and wet my skin with the vapor, my brain whetting into a razor fever by way of the drink, the ocean's breath on my face, a shitty old compact Hondo divided by the dueling mortality of its cargo, blasting into the unknown on a stretch of L.A. highway I'd gone down a hundred times before. I reached into my pocket and thumbed

Hal's unfinished death letter. Though not a suicide, it was a death letter just the same. I reasoned that if I didn't think of something soon before the 10 West bottomed out at the feet of the Herculean Pacific, I'd simply drive straight into it and bury us both.

# Chapter Two

THEY call it June Gloom in L.A., this fog. I could barely see a thing as it was and my eyes too were growing a fine gloss: tears of whiskey and of course the insistent thoughts, the memories. I felt the committed nip of grief and abandonment, yet not so much that I asked aloud, "Why?" Eerily drawn to the ocean, I was rapidly growing romantic about it swallowing me up and finishing the business of life. If I crashed, I crashed, as it were, which is stupid but honest. I cared, but not enough—save for Hal, who I thought should have something more quietly ceremonious. As for my own sake, forget it. Maybe I didn't care. That is until I veered too close to the sloped-V median of the final exit off the 10, the car nearly sliding into the cement foot and then almost crashing into a sedan cautiously trying to cross lanes to the off-ramp. My heart raced off beat. I struggled with the wheel with two right hands. The exit sign flashed at me like a silver switchblade and directly my gut took over. Where the 10 makes an abrupt T into the rim of Santa Monica, I bore down and pulled a hard right at the last moment, making it onto State Route 1, north, the Pacific Coast Highway, with thin tires whining through the turn like wicked children.

It was precisely the kind of aide-memoire I often needed over the past few years. Little shoves of fright geared toward the non-romance of actual death. Legitimate reminders that life was something tangible, corporeal and animal, to be touched and not too insulted with disregard, no matter how bad or ridiculous living seemed. And that was the kind of thing Hal would have said, would have advocated, no matter how bleak his own life was. He had influenced me, maybe he had not ultimately changed me or made me any kind of a better person, but he was there, both the devil and angel at my shoulder sewn up into one tiny bag of conscience. I got my bearings and hit the whiskey, walked the fine line of disregard with it in my throat, gasped, and hit the gas with a nervous foot into Malibu. The fog formed a flat gray wall against the sea. Not a sparkle on its loping surface could be seen. The houses of the Palisades and then Malibu were little more than streaks of flashing dim light built into the misty curtain.

Despite consequence, I still longed to break through, cut through the night like a phantom could, just to feel the salt on my face. If not into the water, I wanted to drive right onto the beach and throttle the car's teeth with sand: and then what? But I was alive, and I began trying to figure out what Hal would have wanted. How silly it was that I could play oblivion against mortality with a dead man in the trunk. Taking life for granted with your old buddy dead and not even riding shotgun is a hard choke. I decided then that north was good, north felt comfortable. Time to think, reason. Forget the sea for the time being. *Take it easy old boy, cool down, keep your head about you*, I told myself, as if it were Hal scolding me lovingly as he often did when I'd slip into savage introspective delirium. The thought was reassuring enough to stay on the road. I eased on the gas, rolled the window up and then back down all the way. Breathed. Yes, slower, cooler. But, then again, six days six days six days ringing softly yet omnipresent behind the place in my ears where Hal's old voice too coaxed me quietly onward...

I'd met Hal a little over three years before. He found me wandering over the 1st Street Bridge with a cast hand freshly minus the index finger, doped out of my mind on a gaggle of legit pharmaceuticals, discharged from the hospital in a gluey miasma only hours earlier. I'd been slogging mystified through the long city streets. I had lost a finger. A true tragedy realized—looking at my hand I could see with solidity the empty space hanging there just after the bandaged nub. Illusory enough, a true mystery unresolved, as if what I had to do was simply find it and all would be well. Convulsing and in a state of dementia—a listed side effect of the antibiotics exacerbated by the opiates—I was convinced that the finger was still alive, writhing with the angry and determined life of a cut earthworm, and being held for ransom by a man named Sweet Julio. An old nemesis of sorts, Sweet Julio lived in Boyle Heights, the Latino borough across the river from the eastern edge of downtown. Find him, find it, and screw it back on. Only partly indulgent, I had never been chiefly privy to drugs prior, at least not enough to spiral out and down with them, and often thought them little more than a sometimes apposite distraction, but a severed finger and a stay overlooked by a crazily jolly Armenian doctor with a liberal sense of dispensation was turning me around. I bought the hallucination, and I bought the hunger.

Ejected from Boyle Heights with no avail re: the finger, I was treading along the middle hump of 1st Street like an inconsiderate suicide, which is precisely what Hal thought I was when he first saw me.

"Hey. Hey, lost dog. Hey!"

I could barely hear him, but I saw him, thirty yards in front of me, leaning on the railing with what looked like an emaciated dwarf. Through the distance and my skewed eyes he and

19

his companion resembled two antique marionettes swaying to and fro in the apex of the day's sun, dancing slowly like golden, happy fools on the bent back of the quiet, otherwise deserted viaduct. As I got closer their woodenness only grew more real.

"Hey, get the fuck out of the road, man! It ain't worth it, and I don't want to see it," he hollered. The sound rolled toward me as loose and adrift as tumbleweed.

"What?"

"You might get creamed is what, and I don't want to see it. So if you could please kindly wait until me and my lady-friend here have departed this ol' bridge, it would be much appreciated."

I was confused and looked it. I had not realized that I was walking the center line after drifting back and forth to the edges, transfixed by the sun casting off and through the shimmering buildings of downtown: the lit star hurling itself down onto the Pacific West, a bright and shameless fuck-you to the cool beauty of the night. I was lured toward it like a fish out of murky water, with a brain only half-tuned into reality. I'd been run out of Boyle Heights and lucky I had not gotten the shit kicked out of me, having wandered relentlessly through the dusty barrio streets and into all kinds of establishments, crazy with longing and blown on top-shelf prescription candy, with curled, dried white lips asking after Sweet fucking Julio and where was my finger and my guitar too and where was Julio's heart so I could put my dagger in it though I was not in fact carrying a dagger.

The folks at the Catholic or Presbyterian or some brand of church merely thought me insane in a harmless clinical sense, a mental case worthy of pity and innocent in the eyes of their Lord, and tried to give me a loaf of bread before sending me on my way. The various shopkeepers mostly ignored me until I gave up, or they threatened to call the police. It was at Lulu's Tavern that danger became me. Not that it's really too sound for a sluggishly mad Anglo to wander any of L.A.'s Latino boroughs calling out to kick the ass of anyone, let alone badmouthing *norteño* as I sporadically did on that day, they especially didn't want to hear it at Lulu's where the jukebox is filled with *Tejano* hits. The only thing that saved me from the small patience and melancholy irritation of four husky Mexican laborers was the bartender who'd studied me through veteran urban eyes that had surely seen worse. He escorted me through the rear and pointed back toward the bridge. Addendum to the hand, he had noticed the stink that I myself had yet to notice coming up from an oval puddle at the cradle of civilization in my pants.

I was released from the hospital with a shot of morphine and the lethal cache comprised of a large jar each of Vicodin and OxyContin, multiple vials of serious antibiotics, and a quart of liquid codeine—a doggie bag full of enough goodies to kill a camel. Of each I immediately disregarded the recommended dosage, ingesting large samples of it all with a few healthy pints of Kentucky bourbon. Despite my prior apathy toward most fixers, I was absolutely and for quite some time no stranger to alcohol, and I was speedily learning the labors of heartier substance abuses. I warmed to the bag of narcotics like a hardened and reckless enthusiast. I needed the medicine, for the physical pain, sure, but moreover to subjugate the disbelief of losing the finger. The barkeep knew better than to take seriously someone shouting cryptic obscenities while wrapped in fresh casting and with a denim crotch wet and stinking from hot urine, so, Thank you, pills and potions and piss, my executors.

When I reached Hal I turned and studied him and the woman before opening my mouth. Both had skin the bluish-white of melted candle wax dried near a recently burned wick.

"Sweet Julio," I said.

Hal squinted at me as if I were a glint of harsh light.

I said, "Where is he."

"Your pardon?"

"Nothing." I tilted some, leaned over the railing, and gazed

21

down onto the coarse concrete of the Los Angeles riverbed.

"Now, you ain't gonna jump. Don't dishonor the lady," Hal said, regarding the dwarf who was not a dwarf, but a slim, dehydrated, yet elegant woman with enough grace left in her face to know that she was once exceptionally fetching. "This is Pam. Little Pam, and I've done spent enough time this afternoon convincing her not to go over. I'd hate to have wasted this day, friend."

"Friend?" I asked.

"Sure, why not," Hal said. "What's the trouble?"

I held up my doctored hand, three fingers and the one thumb left on it.

"Yeah, well, I'm missing a toe. So what? It happens."

Pam giggled, her heavy makeup smeared down from the drainage of what must have been heavier tears.

"The guitar," I said.

"Well, I don't know anything about that," Hal said. "You, Pam, the guitar?"

"I am Pam," she said, "Little Pam."

"Pam," I said.

"Little Pam," she said.

"Little Pam," I said.

"Charmed," she said, holding out her hand. Through the subjective brain stupor I could tell she wasn't entirely straight. I found in her eyes a chemical affinity.

"You pissed yourself, lad," Hal said, as if I had not realized it, which until that very moment I had not. The barkeep hadn't mentioned it. I stared down between my legs and touched the dark stain with disbelief, as if poking at a replica of myself in some future museum of the damned.

"I'm looking for my finger. Someone stole it." I withdrew the bottle of liquid codeine and took an obscenely juicy swig.

"That so," said Hal. With a start he flashed at the bottle, his tongue darting over his lips, fangs coming alight in his eyes.

Little Pam followed in her own wanting kind, an ache not of lust but of pure sad love.

"A guitar player stole it. Sweet Julio. He stole my finger, they gave it to him. And my guitar, too." I put the codeine back into my pants.

"They?" Hal's lips caked with spittle.

"Never you mind," I said, and I scrambled up the railing. I stared off to the north, where the ditch that was once a mighty river bent west, and through the orange glow of sundown I could make out some of the San Gabriel Mountains taking their stand against the city. It was a tremendous scene, the old woody peaks holding their own to the push of commerce, with humankind's own special stink too triumphing—in its ugliness the dormant cold fact that under everyday auspices the byproducts of the clouded farts of industry made life in many ways easier. Or convenient, anyway. That it all has made us live longer, while ironically poisoning us; a tricky thing to reconcile, but somehow in that small eclipse it made total sense, to the point of tears. Some of the finest guitars in the world are made in some factory. I patted the bag of pills and capsules in my back pocket. Imagine losing the finger in medieval times with a hot iron cauterizing your skin, melting it back together with nothing but bitter grog to get you through. I reached my good hand out toward the faint hills, twisting the fingers into an abstract chord and peaking through them as if the crest was the holy machine that kills fascists.

The view would make a suitable portrait for the last thing seen on Earth, if I could subsequently keep my eyes closed against temptation before my skull smashed against the concrete, creating a momentary stain to be partly washed away by the dribble of stagnant water and partly permanent until the rains came—but ultimately to be forgotten. A swan dive would do it, something elegant. I had been a decent swimmer in my youth. Though at the time splayed eyeballs and a cracked brain-

23

case could not be my own special certainty. Feeling light, it was as if I would simply float up as a feather would in enough wind if I jumped, rather than down, where the pathetic trickle of the Los Angeles River stewed its quarry slowly. Baking all it knows in the Southern California sun, waiting for the winter weather to come wash away its cruel memory only to let it suffer again next season, next year and the year after, and so forth. In spite of all the debris the river gathers in its other fifty miles, many a disenchanted soul has jumped from the 1st Street Bridge. The Los Angeles police blotter quit listing the occurrences long ago.

"Now what is this?" Hal said.

"There's nothing doing," I said. "You can't play without it." And quietly I said, "I can't play without it. Now Julio, how now. Now Julio, finally, Julio can really *play*."

"Play, son? I can play. How 'bout I just push your dumb ass over and then go get some dinner." Hal was old. He was around sixty-five at the time, I guessed, and would seem to age a decade for every year I would come to know him. I never found out his actual birth year, but staring at him from my existential perch it seemed to me then and forever that time had been both horrible and kind to him.

"I'm starving," Pam said.

"You eat dinner yet?" Hal asked me. Then he said slowly, with great deliberation, "In order to think straight, you got to eat. No man's head is screwed down the right way until he's had some food in him. Doesn't matter what the trouble is. Liberty, God, truth. Amputation. Whatever. Love, even. Truth, yes. The brain, the mind hungers. But when all is said and done, it is just an organ, same as the heart, the liver," he gushed and groaned lowly to himself, "*God bless the liver*," and continued, "It needs to be fed to take care of business. One has to eat to get on with it. We eat at The Amigo, two blocks over."

The opiates shifted gears, a levy of constipation broke inside of me, and I too grew insatiably hungry, and weak, so weak. I hadn't eaten properly in days, minus the intravenous feed tube at the hospital. A threshold shakily retaining posture beneath my skull fully gave way, and my body fell slack. I slipped from the railing and landed a doomed cowboy astride the iron bar. It took more than a few questionable seconds for the sting to register, longer than it normally would considering the painkillers, but the pain did come, dull and foreboding and chokingly. I grasped my testicles with my one good hand. They were soggy with piss. The other hand I slammed down with soured instinct onto the railing. The agony in my balls was swiftly disregarded as the grisly and unholy, incomparable pain of the taken finger took over. It had not been a clean cut, and it throbbed ghoulishly with the cavernous drum of a death march.

I teetered toward the riverside. So be it, I could no longer cling to anything. Going over this way it would not be face-first that I would flatten from a dive into the bottom below. Most likely bouncing the side or top of my cranium would commemorate a graceless fall from a more graceless time in the world. I went perpendicular to the railing. The bag of drugs slipped out of my pocket and crashed to the ground scores of feet below. In a flash I would have been lucky to hang by one leg. It was then that, as if he had been waiting patiently for a verdict, Hal reached over and grabbed my foot. Holding it, he stuck his hand in the waist of my pants and pulled me down onto the road. His arms were not especially strong, but they were determined, and I guess I owe him no matter how indifferent to death I was at the time and would be off and mostly on for some time after.

I reached out with nine fingers and caught my breath before it chased the dragon on down. Then, by collective instinct, Hal, Pam, and I looked over the railing to where my many pills lay scattered and dissolving. It was a heartbreaking thing to witness for us all, the rare quart of codeine shattered and mixing with the scummy, frothy trail of water indolently making its way south to Long Beach.

Little Pam seemed as if she was going to dive after them. Hal planted her firmly against the railing and tore ass down toward the water, running then scrambling like a man forty years less his age.

"Gone," Little Pam said. The tone in her voice was as if it were a child who had been lost to the river.

We watched in silence as Hal began the fruitless attempt of sliding down into the steep cement ditch. Halfway, he stopped. He sat back on his hands and stared at the dissipating mess. A sea of graffiti surrounded him on the bank, so much so that he seemed as lost to civilization as a spec of mitochondria in an ocean of biology. He stared at the puny trail of water as if there were a great storm for the ages brewing on it, cautious to pull anchor and heave the sail—a good day to die, but not *the* day.

"I think I needed those," I said.

"Boy, didn't we all," Hal said, huffing back up. "You're the worst doper I've ever seen. Bravo. My name is Hal," he said, turning to me. "Hal S."

I leaned my head back and stared into the seamless cobalt blue of the sky at day's end. Sky so clearly blue above but a Van Gogh swirl of orange, purple, and smoky brown when looking straight out toward the hills. "Guitar," I hummed.

"I think I have some trousers back at the pad that'll fit you. You got a name, lad?"

"Yes," I said, "I do." And I stood loosely on my feet before Hal S. and Little Pam took me arm-in-arm back to The Amigo Hotel.

I was wearing those very trousers on the road north, and Pam— Little Pam as she was called—was one of the last people I saw before hauling Hal's dead body out. By the time Hal died he would lose more than a toe. Strange how yesterday can feel so far away yet so close, like an ex-lover, maybe, or blood gone sour. The smell of Hal began to creep up through the back of the Hondo. I reached over and rolled down the passenger window. The steering wheel, dashboard, my hands, and now the seats covered with fine vapor. The fog only grew thicker as I cut up past Malibu and into Ventura County. I pushed into the bend of Oxnard, wanting to get past the point as quickly as possible—and even quicker through Ventura and on to where who knew. I just wanted to be away from civilization as much as possible, no matter how difficult it was to leave Los Angeles and its overcooked human stew. I wanted to leave the fires burning and disappear in smoke.

The bottle of whiskey was wearing thin, but I had another in the trunk, nestled between Hal and the spare and what little else I gathered of his before leaving The Amigo. Even loaded on the grain, I felt more sober than I had felt in a long time and conscious enough to ease more on the gas through the long and dreary stretch of city ahead. It was no time to tangle with the California Highway Patrol. The questions would be unbearable and my explanations surely insufficient. I had designs in my head about redneck cops stomping around Oxnard like senseless ogres, looking to hang me at the county line and feast on the dead.

But where? Being without course can be a hex or a freedom, though at the moment it felt like neither. I did not feel cursed to be riding with the corpse of my friend, and I did not feel blessed. Honored, perhaps, but not enough to have a straight plan of action. Then a thought came to me, a memory. One of Hal's favorite places in California. A somewhat desolate stretch of the PCH just north of San Simeon. He had spoken about a lighthouse there—another of Hal's esoteric interests was lighthouses, he once lived in one—and of elephant seals. The place is Piedras Blancas: "White Stones." A beach full of elephant seals, the elephant seals of Piedras Blancas. I had never been there.

I put the whiskey back to my mouth and set my swollen eyeballs on their course. My own mortality no longer a thing of question, borne now with purpose I prayed I would make it out of Ventura County alive.

# Chapter Three

"YOU gawn eat that?" Little Pam asked.

"No."

"Shit. Them fuckin birds a howlin, make it hard."

"Yes," I said. The birds.

It was the morning I found Hal dead.

The Amigo Hotel sits on the same edge of downtown as the 1st Street Bridge. Tucked away in vacuous desolation where the gut of the city barrels to a halt up against the massive man made ditch of the enervated and sad Los Angeles River, bordered on the south by Skid Row, the west by Little Tokyo, the north by the county prison. A converted old building of brick, sheet metal, and long timber, The Amigo occupies one end of a short block along Santa Maria; a waterfowl slaughterhouse serving Little Tokyo, Chinatown, and Koreatown is on the other. In early dawn the trucks arrive with hundreds of crated ducks and geese. The engines cut, and confused with quaking bills suddenly filled with the death-stench of their own kind, the birds start screaming. They scream for hours until, caged against the nervous, distressed instinct of cannibalism—waterfowl are not wise to suicide, but murder they know—their own numbers are called up to the executioner's blade. Pam's window faced the slaughterhouse loading docks.

"This I'll have, but I cannot fuckin bear to know them birds' terrible song no longer," she said, thumbing a rubbery piece of chicken from a pile someone had left on a half-burned paper plate in the foyer, days old by the look of it.

"They don't kill chickens there," I said. "You're straight."

"Yeah, straight. Ha."

"But safe with the chickens. No cock at the guillotine."

"Thank the heavens, cuz I ain't stomached a nothin since Sunday."

It was Wednesday morning, almost 9 a.m. on June 27th, and the chicken was the only thing she could have been straight about. Little Pam had been on a winder. She was called Little Pam, and it was meant without irony, but what she lacked in size she made up in balls, so to speak. She was indeed a fully realized but incredibly tiny woman. No, not a dwarf, but somehow even smaller in effect, miniature, petite I call it, but she could jack it with the best—and by best I mean worst—of them.

"You been to Boyle Heights?" I asked.

"Sumtin fierce."

East across the river in the same Boyle Heights I had stumbled so worthlessly out of years prior was where the junkie patrons of The Amigo would venture near the end of each month when their social security checks arrived. There they could afford higher-quality chiva than the shit scored down on Skid Row. Shit sometimes meant literally, when some unlucky and jonesing resident would rush back to The Amigo to wantonly fire their goods only to find that they had just purchased with the very last of their precious dough nothing more than a cube of some on-the-Row renegade indigent's petrified excrement painstakingly rolled into a little ball and stuffed into a

30

rubber balloon. Out on a walk once—away from The Amigo I would spend my time walking or driving the vast empire of Los Angeles streets, the network spider thick and knotted in its belly, with a thousand long legs stretched audacious with conquest—I witnessed in perfect daylight a ragged man with a seasoned chef's precision dicing his cooled dung into equal half-inch squares, as if it were a large brown tomato. Assorted balloons lay in a pile next to him. Orange, green, blue, red, and yellow.

"You shar you don't wan none a this?" A flap of crusted but loose skin escaped Little Pam's mouth and slapped the side of her cheek, followed by the crunch of bone in her wiry old throat. She was from the South, but as for being a lady, a belle, well, she must have let that go long ago. If she ever had it at all. She had the distinct pain of being part Creole. Just a touch, enough to linger between a mark and pride. But her accent was of some broader world. She never spoke, to me at least, of any points between an abstract South and Los Angeles, no matter how clear it was that some truly awful baggage hung forever heavy inside that little body of hers. With her free hand she first swatted above her head at flies that were not there while gnats frantically crawled the mound of cold fried chicken. Second, she reached down between her legs and dug with a fever.

"No thanks," I said.

"Christ," Little Pam answered, disgusted by my rejection. She sometimes called me Sire. She thought I was above everyone because I never rummaged through the dumpster or got hooked on the hard stuff: junk, speed, or crack. Eighty percent of the people living at The Amigo were interminable dope fiends. I was merely a drunk, small peanuts in the larger circus of despair. Also, I did not work, either at hustling or a legitimate job. I had lived frugally for five constant years on the road before settling in L.A. and had saved just enough money to get by on for a while. It didn't cost much to live in squalor.

Pam's hands trembled bringing each bite up to her lips and calmed until she was finished chewing, when she would begin to shake again reaching for another piece.

My own hands had been shaking lately. Little, quick jerks. I'd too often ceased to take food with my whiskey. I had woken from the God dream twenty minutes earlier and hazily tramped downstairs to get the morning paper. My body a slim slug and then would come a fleeting uncontrollable tremor. The street was gray and empty, another fog-infested morning of warm listlessness waiting to be burned off, only to roll back in during nightfall. In the slow and rather questionable state, I wondered if the brutal epiphany of my night's sleep had been dealt abroad and that worlds really were going to collide—finally the end of *Homo sapiens sapiens*, and bliss and grief, too. Was there panic across the city or was it all just subconscious projection ill-fated for my own private tumultuous slumber? The planet is after all a ball of fever. Half asleep, I idiotically believed that the *Los Angeles Times* would have the answer. What did I expect: the president on the front page rolling out the red carpet for Jehovah? Zealots double-fisted, wailing, "I told you so!"? I wasn't sure, but the newspaper box was empty, either never delivered to this derelict wasteland corner of downtown on a dreary summer morning, or fifty-cents freeing every copy toward potential stuffing for some unfortunate soul's makeshift bedding. I decided to go talk to Hal about it even though as a strict rule he did not arise nor wish to be bothered before noon and even that was cutting it close to his usual regimented 1:15 p.m. awakening.

"I got to talk to Hal," I said.

"Forget it," Little Pam said, "it's too early." She said, "And get off a you hi-horsey and eat some a this chicken."

"I'll see you later, Pam."

"Suit yourself, Sire." She took the raunchy plate up into her hands and carefully wandered down the hall to her room, to the trilling view of unloaded ducks and geese whose time had come. Before she rounded the hallway she squatted, and for a moment she balanced the flimsy paper of piled chicken in one hand. With the other she pulled up a loosed stocking and clamped it back into a tattered garter with her teeth, the hem of her skirt held under her chin. I did not know it at the time, but this would be my last sight of Little Pam: rolled into a perfect little strung out pretzel of jilting disquiet, caught somewhere perpetually between resignation and determination.

Hal was no stranger to the spike, but he had discipline. He lived to the right of the room I had come to take, on the second floor, across the hall from Bug Wallace. Bug Wallace is perhaps the world's greatest unknown guitar player and an even greater junkie. Bug did not have discipline, not with dope and not with eating. He was the fattest junkie I have ever seen. Maybe one indulgence cancelled out the other. Two negatives making it as they say. Bug technically should have keeled a dozen times over, but no matter how much he put in his mouth or shot into his arm he persevered. He was and was not disciplined with music. He could play like hellfire but didn't do anything with it outside of his little room. He could do Stone McFreed and Skeeter Green, even Skip and Lightnin', often forwards and backwards. He could even do Leon Krabtree and King Jim, and nobody can do that, but I'll say it anyway. When he played himself he owned the cosmos. Even wasted somehow his fat fingers danced with precision on the strings like taut gymnasts. And he did it all eyeless, blind. The Art Tatum of the electric guitar. Bug had lost his vision and a piece of his forehead in the first Iraq War. Hearing him echo through the dim hallway, I had often fallen into thinking about what I would have given to lose an eyeball, even both, rather than the finger, the hand. I had not let on to Bug that, once upon a when, I too played and good. His equal I might say in all humbleness and with due respect. I don't exactly know why I never said anything. The call came from my stomach, out of some kind of shame for losing the finger, as if I had a choice in it. Or maybe it was just too hard to be that close to the instrument again. I was not ready for it. Hal kept my confidence, though he often criticized me for being, as he put it, such a goddamn pussy.

I punched the call buzzer to Hal's room on my way to the stairs. He would be pissed for sure, but now I was feeling urgent: The dream was vivid enough to inspire conversion and it left me bleak, rattled. I'd been properly spooked, a direct contention to my usually staunchly jaded self. I had never been religious in any of the traditional/communal fashions, other than maybe as a minor salve for disbelief. I've long been attracted to the notion that at least religion is poetic, but if you really stop to think about it so are the processes of science. The only difference is in how you play them. As I passed Bug Wallace's room I could hear the soft croon of "All Along the Watchtower," covering multiple versions at the same time. I slowed to hear it, but I did not stop to listen through the wall as I normally would. Bug Wallace the prophet and his instrument the knowledge, religion and science fucking with calculated poetry.

I rapped my knuckles against Hal's door and braced myself for a reproach. Nothing came. I knocked harder. He should have come furious and howling. I ran my fingers over the sign on his door that read: "We don't want any." I spent many nights burning the lamp late with Hal, talking and mostly listening. It had become our little ritual, he the philosopher and I the pupil, King of the Damned and his Courtier of Nothing. We often drank. I always drank. I would leave quietly when Hal took his nod. Hal rarely used in front of me, but he did not hide the facts. He found it odd that the authentic Blues disciple in me had never given over to the brown. He had minor heroes in some of the old-timers but not because of their hand at the guitar. Hal rarely had any other visitors, engaging the rest of The Amigo patrons in the foyer or the common area where many would take their meals—those such as Hal and I who did not have kitchens built into their little rooms. He would spend time with Little Pam in her room. As far as I know they never had physical relations deeper than the needle's plush push. Their romance was the romance of tying on. But the "We" on the sign did not refer to us, Hal and me, but to Hal alone. His demons, his ghosts, too, if you want to look at it that way. More than a figure of speech: specifically, the ghost of his Maggie, her living presence which ceaselessly haunted his life with exacting doom.

I grew concerned. Waking as I did from a vibrant vision of God telling me to shoot myself in the face *today* because the world was going to end next week—it would be all the worse to witness let alone go through, even uglier than splattering the contents of one's head against the already greasy walls of a dismal downtown SRO flophouse—was a bit much, even if all I really had to blame for such conviction was the onset of the d.t.'s. What I needed expressly was some consul, some grounding. Besides, I knew that Hal would be interested. He ate up spiritual juju like a gluttonous mule longing for the pasture. Not to mention guns. At the time I did not know if he had one hidden anywhere in his room. Hal did not particularly *like* guns, but he was crazy for them just the same. It was more of a bona fide obsession than an enthusiasm. He wasn't a redneck. Hal was nothing close to an all-American good ol' boy, despite being from the Midwest. No, his fixations with God and guns were born and bred from a much deeper, darker, stranger place than ingrained ignorance or blind patriotism.

I scrambled back to my own room for the spare key to Hal's room. He had given it to me just in case, despite his meticulous professionalism when it came to heroin, he ever miscalculated and shot a spoon of shoddy dope culled from a bad score. Passing back, Bug had moved on to King Jim's "One Wet Wish, Baby."

The needle was not in Hal's arm when I opened the door.

The room was as stagnant and quiet as the hall of an old museum: a staid quiet, dominating with witness. His stubbly jaw was crooked, hanging down agape as if in an achingly tired yawn. He was sitting in his beloved old herringbone-upholstered lounger. The lights were still on. The air in the room was different, different than even just beyond the door in the hallway. It was stale, and it tasted of bad mustard gone completely to vinegar. Hal was hunched over at the shoulders, but his torso was straight against the back of the chair. It was as if he had only fallen asleep in the position, exhausted. His clothes looked clinging and damp, felled from a storm, cold and shriveled into the chair. Which was not the case. It hadn't rained in Los Angeles since March. Hal had died. I had never been in such an intimate situation with a fresh corpse, but I knew it as soon as I saw him. Like new mothers by instinct recognizing their import, so may we who crawl about in the dregs know by similar nerve impulse the birth of death when we see it.

In life Hal wore an incessant crease along his brow, a permanent ridge of tension and contemplation—pure Neanderthal existentialism—and that was gone. Most likely the clothes were wrung with sweat. It was that one damn thing that you know must one day happen but never really expect it to: It was pure and simple death. By all appearances mostly tidy, except for one piercing unclosed eyeball that stared open and straight ahead, his face petrified into an awful wink, the joke on me.

I looked him over with acute care, tracing his unmoving body from foot to torso, head to chest, arm to arm. I noticed the pen clutched in his left hand and the paper on the floor. For the time being I handled neither. I stared at him for a long while, a full half hour at least, letting it sink in.

Then, in futility, out of ingrained human responsibility I guess, I checked for a pulse and for breath. There was none and likely hadn't been for some hours. His face had begun the death process, already turning to a pasty blue-gray, bluer than

Hal's usual tint, the color of circulated oxygen finally entirely gone from his lips, his cheeks. I put my hand on his hand after checking his wrist. It was cold, no anger left in it. I kept it there for some time, staring at my confidant, a somber smile probably coming to my lips as I thought of the wise old crag and his impassioned armchair philosophies.

"Good luck, old man," I said. I moved my hand to his shoulder.

Hal had taken me in like an estranged cub. He was a vile old bum, but something in him was genuinely kind to me no matter his cantankerousness, and beneath the surface, though void of sentimentality, he was loving. I never really thought of him as a father figure. More like an uncle, maybe. Someone crossed between a much older brother and a grandfather. A hardened sage, and I had come to love him as much as I could. The nights we shared were special, they offered up some needed sense out of life, kind moments within a hidden corner of the general chaos of existence, the chaos of Los Angeles, and moreover the chaos of each of our individual losses and gold aspirations gone south. It occurred to me right then that our times together had given us our days' only peace. It was something, no matter how dreary in reference and parleyed without action it all was. And standing there holding Hal's hand as if he were now an incapacitated elder in a nursing home who I might pull up and help to the bathroom, I felt a vast new emptiness open up inside of me, and I knew that that particular peace we shared was now forever lost. It was the only time I had ever seen the man totally helpless.

I had recently been through the worst years of my life, and Hal in many ways had fed me a lifeline. I'd fantasized so often about death. Now here I was touching it at the source of what had in its own way kept me alive.

I let go of Hal's hand and pulled up the cheap folding chair I would sit on during our nightly discourses. It was a feeble thing with a plastic seat that was oddly comfortable but deceiving, the ass killing with ache as soon as you got up from it. Everything around the room was in its place. I knew with quaint informality all of its detail. Now looking at the stuff I felt like a stranger who'd been away for a long time and was discovering it all anew: the too soft twin bed made up but with the sunken shape of Hal permanently outlined beneath the covers; the three-legged wooden end table with Hal's silk-lined cedar hypodermic box atop it, the immaculately kept antique and oft used needle nestled inside; a velvet painting of a clown with the eyes shot clear out of it; the bookcase mostly filled with religious studies texts, Greek myths, and classic novels of unrequited love; the magazine rack stuffed with wrinkled copies of *Guns & Ammo* beside Hal's chair; the broken and worthless old metal fan Hal refused to throw away; a cheap clock radio.

I slumped into the folding chair. It skidded a few inches across the cracked wooden floor beneath my weight. Mostly I was a bag of bones, but I felt heavier now.

"Hal," I said, "I had a strange dream last night. I'm sorry I didn't come by. I crashed early, and hard. Anyway, this dream. Oh. I'm sorry, too, that I busted in here so early in the morning, but I really wanted to tell you about it. God was in it." I looked over at him, half-expecting his eyes to flash with curiosity, his head tilted slightly forward in contradicted judgment like a Shakespearean king. He would often appear this way when listening. I momentarily forgot that he had no juice left in him for such consideration. It was then that I reached over and with the tips of my fingers shut the one frozen unblinking eye. It shut easier than I thought it would. I gave a little too much force and the end of my middle finger squished into the cornea beneath the lid. Maybe I expected it to be more like hardened clay, but even death takes its own time. I retracted my hand before mashing the eyeball like a large ripened grape into the orbital plate, and I shuddered.

I settled back into the hard seat and folded my hands over my knees. I looked down at them, my hands, expecting a tremble, but they were still.

"We were in the desert somewhere, God and I. It felt like he was holding my hand, the bad one, but when I looked down he wasn't. The desert was like the Mojave but no part of it I'd ever seen. The colors of the mountains shifted before the whole dream went black-and-white: from the dry, dusted browns to a thick, syrupy red. At first, in his image made of man, God looked like a cross between Townie San Vino and Old Bull Lee—kind of like you, actually. It was quite the weathered and carved face." I paused, and I said, "Perhaps it was you."

I'm not sure I would have revealed this detail had Hal still been alive and listening with a conscious heart. Sitting there, the more I contemplated it the more God did indeed resemble Hal, though he definitely was not Hal, or Townie or Old Bull for that matter. For the Devil had his own money invested in riding with the three. In the dream I succinctly knew the entity was something all its own despite playing trickster. I just knew, like old mother death. "It was terrifying, the familiarity, but I shook it off. God was saying, 'I'm just tired, young man, I'm so tired,' over and over again as we walked through the desert. The voice was grave, all sand."

I gazed across the room to the silk-lined cedar box and the focus in my eyes dissolved followed by a flash of pride that Hal hadn't died with the needle sticking out of him. I don't know, maybe it would have been better that way. I don't know how long I sat staring off into nothingness, but when I came to I picked up the piece of paper and read aloud the only thing written on it. I set the paper on Hal's lap. My throat burned like I had taken a shot of shine. Settling back after a deep enough breath, I continued.

"The faraway hills turned to blood, and the sky became a vivid slideshow of total destruction. War, famine, unceremonious and violent cannibalism, with ample time given to each. It was the most horrific thing I have ever seen, Hell's own slideshow clicked by the Lord himself. Mass murder, crop failures, then blood feasts, organ harvests. The total reversal of man. Eyeless people chewing on hearts, livers, guts caked on their chins, with one foot devolving salamander-like back into the sea. I turned and looked at God. He said, 'It's happened enough, hasn't it?'

"I shrugged. Allusion be damned. What could I say? Did God really need me to tell him that, yes, people were the ultimate bummer of creation?

"God said, 'I've tried all kinds of shit out on different civilizations since the dawn of time, and you all fail.'

"'Don't count me in,' I said. 'I am the wolf.' The dream then shifted gears and the color seeped out of it in an upset rushing red river, ankle-deep and seeming to flow without end until the red turned to gray.

"'Don't give me that,' God said.

"'Well,' I said, 'nobody's fault but your own.'

"'Is that what you think?'

"'You should know,' I nodded.

"'Is that really how you think this works? I feel sorry for you, kid.'

"Not sorry enough, I thought. 'I'm not sure it's working at all,' is what I said.

"'What if what harmony exists can only exist because of the cacophony from which it's been raised?'

"'I'd call it The Blues.'

"'What, boy. You think you're better than a dinosaur?' God drew a circle in the dust with his boot. 'It's time for a new ice age. Time to make room for the next species to arise.'

"'Time to change the record,' I lamented.

"'I'm getting sick of playing the same old song,' God said.

"'Sometimes it's not the song, it's the player,' I said.

God wailed, for a long beat he wailed. Then his human form vanished, a fine dust at the mercy of the wind. I never felt as alone as I did in that moment. Though it was a dream, I could feel it. O if a person could be a guitar and a guitar a person."

I looked straightaway at Hal and tried my best to keep my attention on his slack face, speaking to him rather than to the floor, the walls. I noticed his shoeless feet, one hallux and eight toes sticking out. Then I looked at his right hand. The hand without the pen, mutilated a year before. Like mine, but the right. Hal, a lefty.

"Next, God said, 'Hither, sport, I have something to show you.' It was my entire life's events exposed in sequence before me, projected in grainy, ethereal pictures, from my birth in Libertyville, discovering the guitar, the death of my parents, through the rambling days, all of the picking and playing, on up to the present. The finger. You. This place. 'How different it is when we have the fortune of hindsight,' God said.

"'No,' I said. 'It's all the same. I've seen those same ghosts in the bottom of my whiskey bottle. There ain't a single ash of hindsight.'

"'Hindsight's just too obvious for you, saboteur.'

"'Then I'm tired with the obviousness of hindsight,' I said.

"'You'll wake up. Dawn is coming.'

"God was trying to convince me that I had *made* myself lose the finger. He showed it to me—his version, in which I come off like an impulsive boob, like the ghosts of Christmas Past, Present, and Future coiled up into some kind of vicious Truth viper. It made little sense. His thesis about my disharmony was crudely unsupported; for instance, how could dealing with being orphaned at thirteen be a conscious effort in considering future trouble with the finger fifteen more unknown years down the road? All these situations he's saying I threw the wheel, but I wasn't even in the goddamn car. When there is—I

41

say—no such thing as destiny? Did I become so serious with the guitar at such a vital age by dealing with the loss of my parents only to lose it? No. Had my parents become a proponent of a destiny only ordained to flame-out? No. My mother would have shyly pitied God and offered him some milk, and my father, my father would have given the lousy bum five bucks and a cuff on the back of the neck for good luck. The line God was drawing was crooked, but... I had a hard time controlling my thoughts. At a certain point—I don't know exactly how long I stood there eating his shit until it started to taste right—he made me *believe* it all, with a snap of celestial fingers, that there was no randomness, only right decision or wrong decision and in the end consequence, punishment, and/or maybe reward if you're lucky and do right. Which of course goes against pretty much everything I believe in. Then God put my severed finger into the palm of my hand. When I opened my fist the finger was attached."

I rolled my bad hand palm up and looked into it as into an oracle. I had no choice in the loss of the finger. It was taken from me in an unfortunate circumstance, nothing more. Bad fate some would say, though at Hal's deathbed I still did not believe in any kind of destiny, other than the one truth: I was born to play the guitar and nothing else mattered, not even home or woman when it came down to it, nor fate and other such nonsense, not even the concept of God. Such conceit that had finally conspired to rob me of anything even remotely resembling purpose and faith.

One lone tear sprung to my eye and jumped softly down my face, a suicide approaching peace. I looked back at Hal and then again to my crippled hand, still a strange alien thing after long years of slow healing.

"God said, 'Read the leaves, man. Now you are complete, and free.'

"But I did not feel free. Looking down at my hand it felt

foreign still, not triumphant and reliable as it should have. I looked around for my guitar. There was nothing, just me alone in the evaporated landscape, streams of the colorless residue running through my feet with a soft thrash like white noise. I said: 'My guitar, please.' Instead, shapeless and proud, God handed me a shotgun, a slug barrel sawed-off just like you yourself said you used to hunt with back in Michigan.

"God said, 'Rock salt won't do the trick.' Sounded like something you would say. Then he told me to go ahead, it was okay, take it into my mouth like a horse's bit and pull the trigger.

"He assured me it would be for the best. Take his gamble on a new song. There would be no more war, no famine, no cannibalism, but in one week he would simply get rid of this world. And with it, my pain. No more loss, except the royal Loss. No more unrequited love. He did not specify how. A great fire put into motion, maybe. Give the Christians what they want. He said, 'Burning the dead is fine, in fact I prefer it. The ancients were right about smoke, I'll give them that. But burning alive is the worst way to go in case you ever wondered. Far worse than drowning. I'm giving you this chance to do it quick and painless. Even if I do not decide on burning it won't be as easy as this, I promise you. A gun is the best way to die short of just going in your sleep. I even shortened the barrel for you. Bang. Then a little light, maybe. Dark light. There's no time to think once you make the choice, which is a blessing. Believe me. I've chosen to prove you wrong in everything you think you know, and this gun is your consolation prize.' Then he said, 'It's either this or that,' and he pointed to the edge of the desert where the pale horse drank from a neon puddle. It was Los Angeles.

"The gun dangled at my side like a grotesque dead limb, then as honed and gleaming as Excalibur. God formed a luminescent hand out of the nothingness and placed it over my face. In it I caught a glimpse of the exact horror of burning, of

43

the massive peeling of roasted flesh that might come. I could feel the heat on my face. When God removed his hand I woke up, right at the chance to put the barrel to my lips. One week, that's it. Six more days. The craziest thing, the yoke of it all, is that I could smell the desert. I could smell it in the dream. Overwhelmingly so. That's what scares me. It was right there in my nose, in the senses beyond sleep. It was my dream, but it was God's dream, too. And I was hurting bad for the drink. The tremors, the worst it's been. What do you think?"

I sat in silence for some time when Hal's deflating body let out a final gasp. His organs, the lungs, lastly emptying with gravity. It happens, proved by science, not a breath, not a ghost, nothing but lost compression, I reassured myself. Yet it was too mystical to shrug off. Fuck it: Give up the ghost. Let him go. Some would call it the soul escaping. If anyone had it, it was Hal. Either way it didn't matter: I say that was it, one for the road.

"Yeah, I know," I said. "They always sound different when you tell them out loud."

I picked up the unfinished letter off of Hal's lap and folded it. After putting the paper in my pocket I backed away from the body of my once mighty and always troubled neighbor, my friend, my only authentic confidant for over three years going, and I walked softly away, letting myself out quietly and locking Hal's door before returning to my room.

When I passed back by Bug Wallace's he wasn't playing. Instead I heard him laughing through what sounded like muffled wet sobs. He was listening to Major Ulysses T. W. Bluebird, "Gone Down a Time." His crying was unrelated to mine; I was sure that nobody else knew that Hal had died. Otherwise there would have been a crowd, a scene of blathering and head shaking, a commune of debate about another one biting it. The Amigo would have already fallen into a state of mild, medicated hysteria. One more patron gone, and who would be next. No,

44

Bug Wallace was just dealing with his own ends, same as Pam below, same as everyone else in the joint.

I sat in my own room for most of the day and into the evening. I did not own a chair. All I had in my room was a mattress on the floor covered with my wool blanket, a stack of books Hal had recommended sitting next to it, and bottles of whiskey on the windowsill. I sat on the mattress with my back against the wall and drifted in and out of consciousness for hours. I did not specifically pore over Hal dying or even the dream. Instead, I seemed to sit there with something I had known dreadfully little of over time: calm. My hands at rest.

When I came to, the tranquility quickly boiled away into mad recklessness and a hunger for action. For exactly what type of action I did not know. I decided with loose certainty that it was time to leave The Amigo, and all of Los Angeles, and that Hal would be leaving with me. There was nothing left, nothing to work the slow time like hanging out with Hal. The record was over. A chapter had ended. Perhaps some other new one, for good or for ill, was out there somewhere beyond the city limits waiting to be written.

# Chapter Four

WORSE than Ventura is Santa Barbara, a coastal paradise savagely marred by the intricacies of so-called opportunity and haughty tax brackets—an admittedly picturesque but triple latte-fueled Mecca for yuppies of all ages. And now, mere hours before midnight, the freeway running through the city was clogged with traffic and probably had been since 3 p.m., here where the PCH is interrupted by the sometimes graceless U.S. 101. If I had thought about it before leaving, I would have taken the 5 North out of Angeltown to the 46 West through Paso Robles and into wine country before cutting to the ocean and up to Piedras Blancas. I would have sniffed out a map. That is, if I had left The Amigo with any designs other than the ones made by the streetlight refractions distorting through my whiskey bottle.

Was this the kind of hindsight God was referring to? Was I too rash in leaving? Without a strategy had I gambled with bad consequence? Speaking the dream aloud to Hal put me in a dubious state. On the one hand it deflated the impact of the vision and reminded me of true-grit reality. On the other, it made the defining lines of reality itself ambiguous. I was 4/4-guessing everything when what I needed was a new kind of time. Chasing my breath, I decided it did not matter, at least for now. What mattered was getting through this seemingly endless cascade of metropolitan coast without trouble. Even though the 101 through Santa Barbara is separated from the city by drapes of hills and trees I could feel the shadow of bad society looming. I was growing increasingly paranoid with the idea of cops pulling me over, I with an open flagon of whiskey, armed—Hal's shotgun, which I did find—and with a dead man in tow, plus his heroin, which was in the backseat, on my way to perform funerary rites outside of the law. How now, good Lord, do I stand in thine eyes? Get me through this pass drunk and safe, my new God! I started thinking about him watching me. To see how I would handle things since turning down his offer. Not Jesus in the desert, no, not even close, but another son, the one that comes home with his bildungsroman barely alive between his legs.

What lay beyond Santa Barbara—the open road—I began to visualize as victory, freedom. Timely freedom, the kind of freedom that God in his damn eternity probably doesn't understand. And luck. Four hours out of The Amigo and success was measured in small steps, like jigs slowly coming together to complete a larger puzzle that will hopefully be worth the effort. I took the last bit of whiskey into my mouth and sloshed it between my teeth before sending it burning down. I shoved the empty bottle behind the seat as the traffic slowed to a grueling 20 mph. A sea of red glimmered in irregular polyrhythms in front of me. I turned viciously drunk. The rearview blinded with disgruntled halogens. The fog was thinned here. I put both hands on the wheel.

I'd gone back into Hal's apartment at around 7 p.m. I brought the wool blanket my mother made for me when I was a young man, not too long before both of my parents died in a car accident on the 90/94-290 interchange in Chicago, where we lived, where I was born and raised. A big rig taking the curve too fast sandwiched them into the side embankment. Due to the velocity of both vehicles—my father a full-bred metropolitan lead foot—my parents shot up over the safety wall where witnesses said they teetered for one long excruciating second before falling over the Eisenhower Expressway and crashing upside down below, killed instantly. They were coming home from a yearly vacation which that year I had opted out of. I was thirteen—a man, ha!—and after much pleading was allowed to go with my older cousin and some of his friends up to a cabin in Wisconsin instead. In those days it was easy for Illinois minors to buy beer in Wisconsin. Even though they were unsure about letting me go, they were secretly excited. My parents were at the point in their lives when some time alone off in the country romping around like teenagers again could save their marriage.

I was still away when it happened. My aunt and uncle identified my mother and father and arranged the funeral proceedings, a closed-casket affair. Though I was there I could not authentically say goodbye without seeing their faces. The only other memorials I had been to were of much older relatives who had died of disease and old age, looking more like kitschy wax replicates than real people by the time mourners paid their respects at the wakes. With my parents I got nothing but the glossy top of the death vessels, my own reflection staring back at me from the tombs. Considering Hal, the heavenly chemical-infused rays of light slicing through his blinds onto his breathless carcass and lighting up his drawn face like a slumped saint basked in quiet solitude, I regretted never being able to see the bodies of my mother and father despite their disfigurement. I was beginning to learn that true closure came with touch—brushing your living fingers against the flesh of the departed. I was never able to touch my finger after losing it.

Nothing closed. An open case.

I laid the blanket on the floor and put my arms around Hal, hoisted him, and set him on top of it. Rigor mortis was efficient. Hal was already stiff in his seated position. He was shaped like an injured piece of the alphabet, like a Z turned over on its side, or an S made of poor penmanship—or a J that needed to be smoothed out. A holy letter that needed to be smuggled out of the sad book of The Amigo and read in sublime dignity, whatever that was going to spell. I rolled him up and tied the ends of the blanket together and threw it over my shoulder. Hal had a big presence but he wasn't a big man. Not exactly small either, I had to struggle to keep from dragging his set body along the floor.

In the hallway, just as I was about to turn for the stairs, I heard Bug Wallace call from his open door, "That you, Hal?"

"No, Bug, it's me."

"Hey man, how you percolatin'? What that smell?" Bug's nose twitched in the air like a keen rodent's. "That smell like death."

"It's nothing," I said, pushing Hal fully around the bend of the landing and down onto the top stair, where I held him.

"That ain't the smell of nothin', now. I know that smell. You forget I was in a war."

"Rats," I said. "Hal had a couple of dead rats he didn't know about in the back of his closet, cooking in the musty dark in there probably for days. I just come over to take them out."

"Rats, ay. Hal ain't scared of no rats. Why you got to do it?"

"Hal's out," I said. "Downstairs, taking his dinner. I owed him a favor."

"Favor, huh. This late for Hal's supper."

"He skipped dinner, or whatever you want to call it. He was out. Scored last night for the first time in a week, went a little overboard. You know how it is. Hal's a little too tender to deal with rats right now."

"Lord, I do know."

"Well, Bug, I got to get these out of here before it stinks up the whole hallway, including your room."

"Let me help you," he said, coming out.

"No, I got it, okay."

"Let a useless blind man have some purpose."

It broke my heart to hear Bug say he was useless. Despite how hard it was for me to accept this amazing ability living brazenly right across the hall, like horny newlyweds screwing incessantly in front of a widower, hearing him play was together with Hal's company a ritual that helped keep me going and relatively sane. I was the one who was useless. "Don't say that. You're one of the greatest guitar players I've ever heard. If that isn't useful then go ahead and strike me dead here where I stand."

"Yeah, it's gotten me real far," Bug said, waving his arms about. "Shit. What you know about the guitar, I don't want to know."

I was losing my grip of Hal, my palms beginning to sweat. "Listen. Do me a favor. Let me take this out and when I come back I want to sit with you and listen. I mean really sit in your apartment, like an audience. I've been listening to you through the wall for too long, and I want the real thing. Can we do that?"

"Sure, kid," Bug Wallace said. "Them must be some big rats though, I ain't never smelled no rat that strong."

"They're giant," I said, "like an old horse."

Bug laughed, but it was a cynical laugh. He went inside and shut his door.

I did not pass anybody else on the way out to the small lot where I parked my Hondo. The Amigo was mostly quiet. Residents rarely left their rooms. I still hadn't met most of the people who lived there—a blue devil box of a building inhabited by ghosts. I was especially thankful that Little Pam wasn't lurking around the foyer or the front entrance. She and Hal were close, and I felt a strong pang of guilt infest my spine from not going down and telling her what had happened. Who would be there now to convince her not to jump? Hal had many times talked her out of doing herself in. But behind the guilt, I knew slipping him out of The Amigo and into speculative legend would be for the best. Mystery can also keep a person alive. If I told Pam, I reasoned, it might have been enough to make her go ahead and do it. Closure sometimes comes in trumping spades.

I opened the trunk, shoved all of the emptied oil quarts to the sides—the Hondo had three leaks but was otherwise reliable so long as she was fed—and lifted Hal in. His legs curled perfectly around the spare, but his upper body needed to be pulled straight in line with his waist in order to close the trunk. I opened the blanket and reached in, yanking at his shoulders, and straightened the J. Stretching him made a creaking sound like testing old wood. Then I heard a brittle snap. After, I was able to pull Hal into the perfect fit. I did not look in or feel around to find out what had given way. There would have been nothing to do to fix it, and, aside from the grisly sound, it did not seem to matter under the circumstances. Getting the hell out of there was what was becoming mandatory.

I went back upstairs, to Bug's room. He was tuning his guitar, a workhorse of a 1963 Fender Telecaster, the year when the factory covered some of the unsold sunburst bodies with black without stripping them first, Bug's worn at the forearm area where Ra peeked out of the lacquered dark netherworld from years of railing on it. He put it through a homemade distortion pedal and a crusty old Marlboro Sound Works tube amp with a constant hum and crackle that if fixed would be missed. He ran his fingers up the frets. It sounded incredible, like a hot puma saying yes. Like thunder calling down the gods. The guitar had been beaten to the perfect warmth. He sat in a chair across from his bed. I sat down on the floor. It was the first time I had been inside Bug's room, although I had seen it through his open door many times. He had the chair, the bed, his guitar and amp, and a small refrigerator, a stereo with a turntable, and crammed into every other available space were stacks upon towering stacks of CDs and aisles of vinyl records shoved against every wall. The G.I. Bill sold for smack and rock n' roll.

"What you want to hear?"

"You choose," I said. I felt sick, gut wrought with anxiety. Toothaches in my fingertips and no blood in my feet. As much as I wanted to hear him, I wanted to leave. I also wanted to grab the thing out of his hand and do—what?

He said, "Maybe some old Machinatia, *Lord of Pawns,* you know, before they became a bunch of pansies, how's that? Or some Grog Grin. I been rocking some a that heavy shit lately. Or you want to go the other way? Maybe a little Salton Sam, or some Dick Jameson, you know—*Bear Without?*" He riffed the opening notes. "Do you know it?" He hung his damaged eyes on some distant horizon and said, "I can see it, can you see it?"

What do you tell a man with no eyes about seeing anything? "No," I said. A lie. Of course I knew it. It's about a bear.

"Well, shit. I know it. That record give me visions. With my own two ears, I can see it. The fuckin' bear ate him on that one," he said, darting his soft-boiled eyes at me and a quick grin. "Just ate him right up."

"Like God and heroin," I said.

"That record is about California, kid."

"You know Orkhon Korkut?" I said.

He gave me an evil, suspicious look, and it was as if he really could see me with those battle-worn eyes of his, the spongy whites swelling to focus. "What's that, that's Turkish. The only Turk shit I can play is Ali Baba and the Forty." He flashed me again with his loaded face. "Hell. Turkey ain't too far from Iraq, dig? Otto-man. You know, I might be able to play some, but I can't sing that shit. I'm just a dumbass punk from East St. Louis. Not dumb cuz I'm a punk, but dumb cuz I signed on the dotted line, know it." He pointed the forked fingers of a peace sign at his sightless eyes, this signifier of peace shaped like the tongue of a snake. "But we all have our hang-ups, now don't we? Orkhon Korkut. Shit."

Bug was deeper into it beyond anything I could have imagined. Trying to live so anonymously oblivious across the hall, I felt a grand fool. I wondered how a blind junkie shut-in could keep in touch, from the far-out fringes to the deepest foreign Blues. I could not remember the last time I had heard aloud the name Orkhon Korkut, from my own mouth let alone anybody else's, and I filled sickly with a gutshot, worming regret that I had been so scared of carrying on with Bug Wallace, in addition to feeling so apart from myself, for so long. I felt like I no longer knew who I was. Had I ever even played at all? How long had it been? Almost four years: It might sound miniscule in the telescopic void of breathing life, but it felt longer and more unrelenting than any other piece of time I have known, including losing my parents. Sometimes the bears eat everyone.

"I ain't assumin' you got all day."

"'Goes Down the Devil Brave with Love,'" I said. Bug could do the others, so many others, but he did King Jim best, and with exacting passion. Which is a lot to say because because because nobody can *really* do King Jim, most make superb asses out of themselves trying, yet somehow Bug Wallace could do it.

"Sure as shit, that ain't no cop-out. Some folk call it cliché to say ol' King Jim was a bad motherfucker from outer space—to say he was the best is what I'm sayin', that he is the best, know it...well, fuck 'em."

With that Bug Wallace cranked the amp and let himself go. It was stupefying. Bug's eyeballs were ghost owl white with blown blue irises, the eyes of a bloated old fish came alive as he moved through the first half of King Jim's masterwork. Mowing on, the stark orbs rolled into the back of his head and he sang the words cut with a hunted heart and with chilling exhaustion. When he hit the crashing solo halfway through and burned it down to the end it was almost too much and my own hands were trembling—now far more violently than those morning alky shakes—with the urgent hurt for the fix. Later, thinking about my hands, I thought: So that is what it is to be a junkie. I've known all along. Bug finished with something like an air of hot smoke streaming from his hulking, sweaty frame. I tapped him on the shoulder.

"Play something of your own," I panted.

"Sure, sure," Bug hesitated. Then he went into it, a sonic mind-destroyer hovering in a risen place between The Blues and articulate, determined, and demented noise, screaming above the wonderful discord what sounded like, "This'n for Hal, this'n for Hal..." but I couldn't be sure. He was hammering on the ragged Fender a primordial sophisticate, an unhinged caveman bored with physics and angry at the sun. Sweat poured down his face. It went on for a few minutes, an unbelievable pounding, the strings wailing out divinity's delight yet laced with the torture of the abused, in my mind channeling some agonizingly exquisite and dissonant guitar underworld as the instrument was mauled into a hellish chanting. Bug's mouth twisted up into a scowl of unrepentant purpose, now voiceless.

I rose and backed out of the room. I wanted it to ring in my head as I fled, without interruption. But when I got to the doorframe Bug stopped, the last note hanging wild in the air like a dire wolf snapping before the awful moon.

"I guess I won't be seeing you," he said.

"Well," I said.

"You don't need eyes to know things that surround you are headed for a change."

I fumbled. "How. Do you know what you want to listen to?

I mean, you know. Without reading the labels, the, cover art."

"Who the fuck cares? How do you know Orkhon fuckin' Korkut?"

"Hal told me about him," I lied, a blatantly stupid lie, so soggy with obviousness that I almost punched myself in the throat out of shame. To lie the worst of lies is to approach, however audaciously or in the cold sweat of survival—a sore pinch for bravery, and too often a poor substitute—the badness of politics.

"Bullshit. You used to play. Ain't no cracker-ass drunk know shit about any of what you know without *knowing*, dig? Asides, Hal don't give a shit about this, he don't understand playin'. He don't know fuck about Turkey, his head so far up the ass of Jerusalem. All Hal know and care about is the plunger. Plus, I got a gut. Not this one," he said, grabbing the robust drum that was his belly and shaking it. He pointed to his temple. "A gut, you know, here. Don't take it for granted that I'm blind. I got a bloodhound nose and the ears of a goddamn bat. I hear what you guys talkin' on the other side of the hall. On top of that we can smell our own, can't we? And you stink like a player, too."

"So," I stammered foolishly on in full cop-out, "how do you. Know which CD and record. Is what?"

"You want it to be like that, huh. Hal right, you goddamn soft. Okay. I got a secret. You tell me what you hidin', and I'll tell you what I'm hidin'."

I felt a bad jolt clip the small of my back and run like a greasy rat up my spine. I covered my bad hand with the good. "What do you mean?"

"I've smelled enough rat in my life, see? You give Hal my condolences, okay."

"Sure," I said. "I don't know what you're talking about."

"Awright, awright. Then why'd you quit?"

I stopped breathing and said nothing.

"Come on, man. I know what you coverin' up. And it's just

sad. We could be tight!" He held two fingers close together and tapped his nose.

Exhale. I had to let go of one lie before I could bury the other. "I don't have an index finger. On my fret hand." I raised it to him as if he could see it. "It was chewed off by a dog."

"Damn. I am sorry. A dog?"

"A police dog," I said.

"Here, in California?"

"Yes," I said. "Here. In Los Angeles."

"Goddamn. I mean, a dog. So much for a best friend."

"If I ever had one."

A portion of silence was split between us.

"At least it wasn't a bear," Bug finally said.

"Yeah. It was a dog," I said.

"You can get around that. We all dogs." Bug held out the guitar. "Django, Iommi. They got around that shit. Hell, that kind of shit made them what they were, working they gimps into something nobody could touch," he said.

I cringed. It was the very pep talk and with the very axemen that no matter how sincerely delivered I did not want to hear, that in itself had partly kept my secret in earnest. Django Reinhardt and Tony Iommi moved their playing forward with their losses, but I had not in my own mind found any single conception that would make playing without my left index finger progressive in any way. And without progression, without pushing the picking and the playing forward, there was not a goddamn reason in the world, or at least in my heart, to mess around. I could jam in my head, but playing, *really* playing, had been buried in so much misery that it had become obsolete. Which is quite sad considering that it was all born from the simple joy of fingers on strings excited toward the simple magic of sound.

"You want to check it?"

"No," I said. I slammed Bug's door behind me without saying goodbye. As I scrambled back down the stairs I heard him crying after me.

"Sometimes I can see, little brother. Sometimes I can see!"

In the backseat of the Hondo lay Hal's hypodermic box. Inside of it were his antique rig, a Zippo lighter, silver spoon, and a sack of wadded heroin. Some of his other things I put in the trunk before dragging him down and ultimately leaving The Amigo. Clothes, the clown painting, the cushion from Hal's chair. A sawed-off slug-barrel shotgun. I found it in the ratless closet and scared shitless I dropped it into a paper sack and ran it down. I left the crappy old fan and the alarm clock. From my own room I grabbed only the whiskey. When I finally got out of Santa Barbara, after reuniting with Highway 1 past the Lompoc Peninsula, I pulled over and retrieved the other bottle out of the trunk. I sent the empty one sailing into the dust of the brunette hills buttressing the highway. The moon was high. I did not snap at it. Instead, I gave it the finger and poured the whiskey into my throat in a steady flume until I gagged and puked all over the turnout and all over my shoes, too. Back in the car and into high gear, I could feel beads of the spew in my beard which I picked out and let into the wind all the way to Piedras Blancas.

I arrived after 2 a.m. I parked behind two large boulders at the far end of one of the turnouts for viewing the elephant seals. There were a few wooden info signs about the seals that I did not attempt to fully read. There wasn't much fog, but it was very dark. It had gotten darker the further north I traveled. Here, clots of black cloud covered the lit moon and blotted out the stars. City lights were long gone. The lighthouse, one of the few built on California's Pacific coast, was a towering pale gravestone in the distance, no longer alight, no longer in use. It was blocked by a gated road obscured by the night. I let my eyes adjust, and I could make out piles of slab beyond the white rocks on the sand where the beach rolled up into brush. Some sections of the slab were jagged stones belched up from the sea in a time before trash—in a time before people—and some of it was smooth and rustled and moaned lazily in the night: the elephant seals. Any darker a night and rock and mammal would have become indistinguishable. I tramped down to the beach just beyond the rookery. A salty salute to the sound of waves, I did give.

At the foot of the ocean I stared out and no visible line between the black water and the black sky could be seen. It was just a black hole. The two planes stretched into a vast unknown horizon of which I perhaps in that exhausted moment had no right to conjure. Hours before, I would have longed to be thrown into it, tumbled like a stone, judged by the tremendous power of the deep in the last unconquerable place on Earth, to be deemed precious and swallowed forever into its cool mystery, or spit back upon its beleaguered beaches with the rest of the litter. Now I felt too small to even justify contemplating it. I stepped up to the water, the tide low, waves lulling the primordial metronome. No big breakers, I dipped my hands in. Smoothing the salt through my beard, I washed my face, then my arms, the back of my neck. I gargled some, spit it back. It was the perfect place. I remembered Hal talking about it:

"Piedras Blancas. 'White Stones,' you ever been there? It's named for the giant white boulders out in the water. There ain't enough lighthouses in California. That's one of the beauties, up there. It was built for a whaling station, back when whaling was something. It's a long, dark flat piece of coast and there aren't any tall cliffs to ward off the ships. It reminds me of the old country. I used to live in a lighthouse on Lake Michigan, after I worked the fishing boats there. I worked the lens. I'd fish during the day, work the lens at night. It was magnificent. It'd be a nicer place than The Amigo to retire, but I can't go back. The lighthouse at Blancas was decapitated in a storm a long time ago. I went there, tried to claim it, take it over, fix it, and work it once again. The 'Pals of the Lighthouse' beat me to it. They don't know anything about lighthouses. Lighthouses aren't for pals. They're for old lone fools who've got nothing left for them but the sea. It's the last time I tried to leave this godforsaken Los Angeles. The last time I tried to do anything with myself.

"There are elephant seals there, too. An ungodly beast, the elephant seal. They're fat, lazy fuckers, but they can move if they want to, and they're mean. Mean as hell. And for that I respect them. They can run, wobbling as they do, faster than a human on sand. Fine company for a lighthouse keeper, the sonsabitches. They don't give a damn. They were driven to Piedras Blancas off their islands. They were overpopulating the islands off the coast, fool mammals just like people, they don't know when to give up. I guess I don't blame them. They were at one time driven to the point of extinction, and once you start fucking your way back to life, it's not an easy thing to quit. Perseverance, the will to endure—the will to procreate, to live forever in the only way possible—it gets in your blood. Elephant seals are not immune. They're pinnipeds. Closest living relative is a bear. Would you believe that? A goddamn bear. Vicious creatures, elephant seals. Have you ever seen an elephant seal molt? It's disgusting. They call it a 'catastrophic molt.' They drop all of their hair and dead skin like a pile of shit on the beach. Terrible beasts. But that stretch of land, Piedras Blancas, it is something remarkable."

It was not the only time I listened to Hal talk about lighthouses, but it was the only lighthouse he ever referenced outside of Michigan. It was however the single time I heard a dissertation on elephant seals. I never knew exactly what Hal's last wishes were. I assume they probably involved some kind of resolution with his lost Maggie, but this place was special enough for him to have mentioned it with passion, and it did indeed seem lovely, though in the shadows I could not see the white stones out in the water for which the place was named. It was convenient, too: Here we were. It would do.

I found a spot thirty yards between the water and a short outcropping separating the beach and the elephant seals from the parking lot and the highway beyond. I smoothed out a bank of sand against the wind and climbed up the slope and pulled down some of the dried, windblown brush. I made a bed of it and then returned to the car and opened the trunk.

I dragged Hal down to the bank and sat him upright. I untied the blanket. His face was caught forever in the gape. I turned him so he faced the ocean. I stuck my thumbs above his eyelids and gently tugged. It felt like the skin was going to rip and I decided not to reopen his eyes. He'd been here before. I was the one who had to see it. Hal was smelling worse. It wasn't cold enough to slow the clock and riding in the trunk wrapped in wool probably helped speed up the processes of death. Whatever had snapped earlier I would leave to the hereafter to fix. I stuck my hands in my pockets and stared out to sea.

"Well, Hal. This is as close as I can get to giving you a proper burial. But you deserved something. I'm guessing you could've died happily in the lighthouse if possible, but it ain't, and that's life. As you know it. I hope this is close enough. I know I never properly thanked you for pulling me off of that bridge, or taking me in, or even lending me these chinos after I pissed my pants. And, of course, all of our nights together. You were an ornery old sucker, but you were a friend, and I appreciate that. I hope this goes to show it." I looked down at him, his head poking out of the blanket like a scared and sacred turtle, a contradiction to the bold, hot-blooded casualty of passion that he was in life. I rubbed my fingers through my beard before returning them to my pants pockets. "Well, thank you, Hal. Good luck in Valhalla," I said, and I turned him over onto the pile of brush in the makeshift trench.

I walked to the car for Hal's box and a pint of motor oil. Back on the beach, I doused the heap and took out his shiny silver Zippo lighter. For what it's worth, I hummed a prayer. Then, producing a flame, I let it go onto my wool blanket, lighting it and my old friend on fire.

Just before sunrise I stomped the smoldering embers and tossed the remains into the ocean, all putrid dust and small pieces of bone, my friend in salt. The whole event took less time than I thought it would. The human body burns fast. Faster than you'd think, especially helped along by 5W-30. I fled from the licking flames and watched Hal burn from a distance, going up into the night in a column of blue smoke. Many cultures believe the smoke from the burning dead is contaminating to the living body and the soul. I just couldn't stand the smell of blistering flesh. It stinks like God. Otherwise, in my isolation I may have been tempted to breathe it in. To breathe Hal in, to host a flash of his ghost. To get from his death what I needed in life. Instead, I safely watched the yellow, orange, and red smack at the dark, the elephant seals moaning in protest or anger or fear. Then the blue. Afar enough, I could not discern in the sacrifice the horrors of burning that God had spoke of and had even shown me a glimpse of. It looked rather tranquil from where I stood. I imagined that if Hal were burning alive it would've been about the same, that he would have taken it stoic, leaving no quarter, no whimper for the ferryman. God was discounting the dead in his pain equation, anyway.

I only left my spot once. Noticing my nub in the pale cataracts of split moon battling the fire to illuminate the night, I plugged my nose and ran into the smoke and retrieved the bones of Hal's left index finger before they turned forever to consummate dust. I cooled and washed the hot bones in the ocean, dried them on my shirt and put them in my pocket.

Now, washing again in the tide, the ceremony over, it was time to take my leave and let Hal and his beasts rest in peace.

Where I would go next I could not conjure, and I swelled with a colossal desolateness. Morning was coming and soon with it sightseers. Tourists. There was no time to linger trying to figure it out: where to go and what was I doing. The light in the tower shined for one slow pulse then went back out.

The elephant seals were coming alive, barking and humping, nipping at each other. They spread out along the beach. After throwing what was left of Hal into the water, I noticed they had crept not more than thirty feet from the path between me and the car. I eyed them cautiously as I made for the road. They were the only witnesses, not to be trusted. They raised and lowered their heads like bulls, their bulbous trunks flaring. Some were fifteen feet long. When I got halfway to the Hondo a gang of them grew fiercely alive and started to charge me, growling at my heels with fat mouths full of mad froth, bucking over the sand like limbless primeval monsters. They were fat, but they were fast for it. The only thing that saved me was a small head start as they chased me with fury across the golden beach. I scrambled up the ridge and turned, watching six of them trying and failing to follow me, flopping back down onto the sand in dull thuds, blubber shaking in the cool dawn, baring their teeth like dogs.

"Maybe in a few million years when you've got feet, you bastards," I said. "Evolution comes slow, but it comes, God willing." I stuck my hand out at them, spanking the crisp morning air, and one gallant beast thrust itself up and almost took my arm off. I could feel the wind slicing through its hideous jowls. I walked toward the car. "Take care of Hal," I said, waving them off. "Watch over him."

Then, turning to face them, I added, "Please."

It was their beach I had violated.

# Chapter Five

I was bit by a wolf when I was twelve years old. I never told Hal about it, and I never told Hal that I had been to Michigan. I did tell him all about my parents and Chicago. My parents liked to go camping every year for the family vacation, usually in rural Illinois or up to Wisconsin or Minnesota, and sometimes Michigan. Once we went up into Canada. My father was crazy for lakes and especially rivers. He liked to fish. He was a bass man, and he was a trout man. He liked to sit listlessly for hours in small, quiet boats. Rowboats and canoes. He liked the peace of it. My mother enjoyed the woods, too, the campfires, cooking out, going for hikes, as did I. The easy wilderness was for us a necessary break from the feral city. What I loved most about it was the swimming, and, as terribly hokey as it may sound, playing guitar for my folks around the fire. We all looked forward to it, two weeks out of each year spent with the serenity of northern forest. The summer before my parents died we took a trip to Michigan, to the Manistee National Forest. We went canoeing on the Little Manistee River, and I got to swim in four different lakes.

One afternoon ten days into the trip, while my mother and father napped beer-bloated and stuffed full of fat fresh-cooked bass, I took a walk alone to go looking for wildlife. Mostly we'd see deer, raccoons, red fox, muskrat, beaver, turkeys, turtles. One time, a wolverine. I tried to keep my eyes peeled for snakes but never found any, save a few garters and once in Wisconsin a northern water snake. My father teased me, telling me it was a water moccasin and that if I spent more time swimming than fishing it would get me, which of course was a lie because water moccasins do not exist in Wisconsin. I did see one years later while camping out on tour near Horse Cave, Kentucky. My father was always on the lookout for bears, that was his nature dream, to see a bear in the wild Midwest, but it never happened. His favorite animal was the bear, and he swore one day he would make it back to California. He always used to say that California was a bear, *the* bear, the only bear in the Union. He used to take trips out west with his uncle when he was young. My father loved bear because when he was out hunting once as a teenager he stumbled upon one—he swore it was a grizzly—and the bear slapped him across the face. Slapped him, he said, just like a father would slap his ignorant son to make him wise. Then the bear just walked back into the woods, grunting. My father said he became a man that day. About an hour into my walk, hoping to find snakes and especially hoping for a bear so I could taunt my father with witness while he was passed out, I instead stumbled upon something far more exceptional: a gray wolf.

The only thing rarer than *Canis lupus* would have been to happen on *Puma concolor*, a cougar. Both had basically been eradicated from most of the Midwest, the cougar more so. At the time it was estimated that less than twenty gray wolves existed in Michigan, so scarce that they no longer roamed in packs. I was walking through a dense part of the forest, all thick underbrush, hoping that I wasn't going to get poison oak like I had on other misadventures, when I came around a large black spruce and there she was. I say she because I could hear the wolf's pup cry in a soft squeak a few feet away.

She stood on her haunches, ridges of thick smoky fur rising in ripples from her neck and rolling in a wave down her back. Before I had even a second to think or react she clamped her warm jaws onto my leg. She held me there, her prisoner. In disbelief, I could not feel the pain. I had never seen a wolf before, not in real life, but I knew it was no dog. My cousin had a purebred Akita, a splendid creature that paled in comparison to this. She did not tear into me, did not rip at my flesh, but just held me there in the vice of her maw. She was trying not to take anything unnecessary from me.

She raised her eyes to me. They glowed like holy moons. Whatever I was feeling—surprise, shock, disbelief—melted away as her eyes held my own. Caught in a psychic handshake with the majestic animal, it was one of the few experiences in my life prior to the dream and aside from paramount experiences with the guitar that I would constitute as authentically religious in any out-of-body sense. It was as if I could see with total lucidity in that moment what it means to exist in the world: the precise balance of it all, wild mammals pushing their luck in the vegetable kingdom. She locked onto my eyes for what could have only been seconds, but profound seconds they were, and then she simply let me go. It was not an attack but a defense: for the pup, I presumed, and thankfully in her eyes I must not have posed a threat. She disappeared with her offspring with the swift escape of a chameleon, retreating into the refuge of deep woods and leaving the unarmed youth of me wholly mystified.

I caught my breath and looked down at my leg. It had two deep puncture wounds. Blood pooled at the openings and dripped slowly down. The wolf had used only two of her four canines. As the amazement waned I filled with pride as if I had passed some important test or rite of passage. Escaping death for the sake of future Blues. I still felt no pain for the first half of the walk back to our camp. Then it came, and punishing. I would feel this way again when my parents died, and again (and again and again) with the finger. My leg stiffened with jolts of ache bolting up from the bite, through my groin, and right into my chest. When I came hobbling toward the tents my father, half-cocked, started to scold me for wandering off without permission but stopped short when he noticed my sneaker soaked in red and my face sunken white. Later, the holes in my leg shadowed with bruise that lasted for months.

That was the last vacation I took with my parents. The wolf was likely another reason they let me go with my cousin the following year, perhaps thinking that I was still traumatized and associating the incident with our annual trip when secretly it, aside from playing the guitar, had been the most fascinating thing I had known in my twelve years. Later in life I wrote two songs for them, my mother and my father, which I kept in my repertoire for many years: "Kin" and "Water Moccasin and No Bear Blues." For the wolf I wrote "Two Hole Punch."

I started playing the instrument when I was six, and I knew from that early age that it was what I most in the world wanted to be: a guitar player. I started playing gigs when I was fifteen in garage punk bands, doing basement shows and parties. I switched to playing solo when I was eighteen and immersed myself deep into dark acidic folk Blues, deconstructing them, rearranging them, trying to push the tone and rhythm and arrangements of them, always trying to do something new while keeping the old authority locked in the light, an obsession that lasted for a decade. I have and always will be an only child, and mixed with the lupine lore I acquired a handle: Lonewolf. It was a good guitar player name. I played under that name until moving to Los Angeles and into unsolicited retirement. I did a few small tours at first, solo and also in a short-lived ugly and brutally awesome metal band called Werewolf—a glorious assemblage of heavy post-adolescent folk art. When I turned twenty-one I left Chicago, left everything I owned except my guitar at my aunt and uncle's house, where I had lived after my parents died and until I turned seventeen, and I hit the road with no limit in sight.

After being on tour for six years straight I decided to rest. I needed a break, and I needed a home. Being on the road constantly means being homeless, and I was tired, so tired. I chose L.A. because it was clearly the most insane and intriguing city I had ever been to, in the U.S. or abroad, though much of Europe and Latin America was tempting. Los Angeles had the right kind of brilliance mixed with the right kind of grit to make it seem like an interesting enough place to lay low for a while. Inspired anonymity. It was in the bowels of the bear, California. It was the West. I always toured east to west, it was my voodoo, for no particular reason other than it felt right. The older I was getting, which was not really old at all, the more I was trying to follow my gut, and my gut was telling me to take five. It was not a simple decision. No matter how much you long for a home and for regularity while on the road it is difficult to settle down. Rambling gets in the blood. Even when you know it's time to take a break it's hard to choke back the shakes. The itch to keep moving, doing it as much as possible while you still can. I rented a small, cheap bungalow apartment in East Hollywood, a few years before ending up downtown, and tried my best to relax.

Sweet Julio was a colleague of mine. We used to cross paths while on respective tours. Julio's home base was L.A. He played in a number of bands, mostly hard psychedelia and experimental punk. He was a master of pedal manipulation. He was also big into *cumbia*, *festejo*, and *norteño*, and a lot of other traditional Latin and South American stuff, which he wove magnificently into his sonic tweaking. His father was Mexican and his mother Peruvian, he was brought up on syncopation and heavy rhythm,

67

and in his prime he distorted it all to a wonderful hell. When I mounted the Angel we'd do small shows together under assumed names for the sheer enjoyment of playing. Blood People, Gnarwhal, Cleetus Young, Catfish Nugget, Future Skulls, Fucking Proverbs, The New Dogs, that was all us. We'd try to one-up each other at every gig, a little healthy competition and jovial ball-busting, it was fun.

Sweet Julio was also neck-deep in the party side of things. He took a bad turn. His recent band was on permanent hiatus but his chemical intake was at an all-time high. He somehow got involved in the dealing side of things and then became a police informant for corrupt cops, hanging out with cheap gangsters and rotten amigos, Mafioso club owners. He definitely had enough talent to make his mark, but even some of the most revered musicians barely get by, especially those who maintain at all costs the freedom of artistic dignity, as we strived to do. Plus Julio had grown up in a poor L.A. ghetto and he'd rolled a certain way when coming of age. Thuggery was in his blood as much as music was. Just one of life's vindictive ironies: Playing guitar got him out of the rough, and struggling to get by on playing music tossed him back in with the sharks whenever there wasn't enough money to go around.

Sweet Julio took to spastic fits and brooding. Even when he played it showed. Something wasn't right with him. A sweaty rubber ball of paranoia, he did not seem to take pleasure in or get anything from the music anymore. Our merry gigs turned sour. Julio was taking them, along with everything else in his life, to some jittery, shadowy place. He started to get aggressive with me when we played, borderline sinister. He grew defensive, even though in those last days he was playing rather like crap. Sometimes he would apologize, but mostly he was becoming a hostile, pompous asshole with acute neurosis. He was getting into speed, dipping his hand in the till of what he was dealing, his forehead an endless wash of sweat and his temples swollen and simian. The ups and downs were unbearable, and I decided to stop gigging with him altogether. Julio took it as an offense, but I shrugged him off. In the animal order of amplifier law, we were guitar players, we weren't friends.

We booked one last date together in Echo Park and Julio did not show up. Nobody had heard from him in weeks. I played two sets, both of our allotted time, and it was fine. I did not miss him at all that night. It was the last show I played. As I was leaving the club a police van sidled up to the curb and two beefy plainclothes officers who looked more like unremarkable steroid-fueled football jocks flashed their badges. They arrested me for no discernable reason.

"Where is he," they asked. "Where is Sweet, and where's the brick?"

They cuffed me and threw me into the back of the van along with my guitar, a Guild M20 mahogany solid-top, my baby so to speak, that guitar and I had damaged each other into the perfect harmony. The cargo space in the van was partitioned into three holding cages, one large one for criminals, two smaller ones in the back for dogs. One of the smaller ones was empty. The other housed a pacing but reserved large German shepherd. In between the cages was a rack of riot gear with bulletproof vests that read "K-9."

The two men, shouting and full of threat, ran me through a course of outrageous questioning that made absolutely zero sense. These were Julio's guys, dodgy cops cut into the Eastside drugs-guns-and-money scene, and apparently Julio had stiffed them something gargantuan. They accused me of being in on it with him, covering for him. They claimed that they "had been watching me for some time." A telltale lie, their mouths spewing garbage loaded with devices as if it were a bad movie. To say that crooked cops exist in L.A. would sound like an embellished ten-cent cliché if it weren't so unfortunately and unapologetically true. In the City of Angels live devils too, some with licenses, where the LAPD shoots—and kills—thirteen year old kids for joyriding and sixty year old women for brandishing screwdrivers in defense from eviction. There exists a hidden layer of bad seed, a deeper, darker grit that I wanted no part of. The city's fantastic noir legacy is an enigmatic draw until you actually become a part of it.

I demanded to be released, standing firm on my ground that the whole situation was complete nonsense and confirming with them for the umpteenth time that their wooly demands were lost on me, that my only association with Sweet Julio was as a musician alone. One of the apes removed my guitar from its case and molested it with painful, brute plunking, breaking the high E string and knocking the headstock into the dash of the van, while the other threatened to smash it all over the sidewalk, or, better yet he concurred, against my face.

It went on for some time, verbal jousting back and forth, in ill resolve. The dog was getting agitated, growling and pacing faster. Barking a foot from my face. One of the officers got into the pen with me while the other drove the van a few miles to the dim lot of a gutted convenience store on Normandie. Parked, the driver joined us and with both of them sitting nearly on top of me, their stale breath wetting my face, a hand each on my thighs, we went through the whole rigamarole again. The thought crossed my mind that they were going to rape me. I'm not sure what they were on. Whatever it was, they were not in an abstemious state. Each wore a pulsating forehead, webbed red eyeballs, and popped wire veins rising from the neck. They took off their shirts. These men were not of sound mind. Their sweaty backs stuck to the vinyl seats of the van and ripped like Velcro as they stirred about. And they were talking fast. I had nothing to offer them. I could not even lie to get the ordeal over with because I did not know a damn thing they were talking about: Sweet Julio stealing a brick (of what?) from a rival cop so these two could send him down the river, thereby claiming the other crooked officer's turf for themselves, only Sweet Julio didn't come through and is suspected to be in cahoots with this other cop to bring down these two's whole arrangement which took years to build—this is what I picked out and pieced together from the frenzied questioning, and it all seemed so stupid and made-for-TV. *Goddamnit Julio, what does this have to do with music? What does this have to do with playing the guitar?* Again, I tried to get them to understand that they were wasting their time. One of them brushed his thick cop hand against my cheek. The other withdrew his gun from the back of his pants and touched the barrel of it to the base of my neck. Then they removed the cuffs and handed me my guitar and told me to play a song.

"We missed the performance tonight. We tried to make it. Oh, we tried. Got there too late."

I did not want to play the guitar. A rare feeling, but I went along. It swiftly occurred to me that I should avoid getting shot at all cost. In Los Angeles there is often no obligation for the dead. I decided, albeit with cynicism and hope against irony, on "Werewolf is the Law," but halfway through, soon after the lyric "The moon is too low and white to hide / Blood in the teeth is the law tonight," I filled with total despair, and total fear, too, and went into hard howling "Rake," followed by my own "Until the Bottle Runs Dry" (*I ain't gonna lie / I'll stay 'til the bottle runs dry*), without breaking between. These songs. Two beloved. I did what I could without the high E, improvising, and I don't think it mattered to my interrogators anyway. I must have played for nearly ten minutes while the goons stared on with immoral grins on their gluten lips. When I finished they did not applaud. Instead, they took my guitar and locked it in the empty dog cage. The German shepherd sniffed at it through the bars, its jaws now dripping with the white drool of excitement. Licking its chops, some of its slobber flicked between the cages and streaked down the body of the Guild and into the sound hole.

"Do you want that to be the last song you ever play?" one of them asked.

The other said, "People pay you for that shit?"

Damn the rhetorical questioning, of course I did not want it to be the last. I wanted to play as far into the future as my body and my intuition and invention would allow. I said, "They don't pay much."

"We just need a little help finding our mutual friend. The girl at the club, the ticket woman, she told us you and Julio are tight, real tight. Said you covered for him tonight. She said you been keeping him cool around there. Said if it wasn't for you Julio would get blackballed from the place, never to play there again. We're going to give you one more chance to—"

I did not let them finish. "Jesus Christ, I don't know anything. I don't even know where Sweet Julio lives these days. We get put on the same bill, that's it. We play, then we go our separate ways. That woman at the bar doesn't know what she's talking about. I don't know—" Before I could complete my sentence they dragged me outside and to the rear of the van.

The German shepherd was growing aggressive with the intensity of it all. Opening the back doors, they grabbed my hands and started screaming, "Talk or pick. Talk or pick one. Pick one. Pick one, motherfucker! Pick one!"

I did not know what they meant until they took the index finger of my left hand, the fret hand, thee golden fucking goose, and shoved it through the mesh in the dog's steel cage. Before I could get a sound up to my throat and out of my mouth, they commanded what sounded like "sickle," and, while the towering men held me with ease against struggle—though struggle I did—the German shepherd took my finger into its teeth and in the first bite pulled the nail and the skin and muscle up to the middle knuckle right off. In the second bite it took the length almost up to the hand off.

72

The dog chomped, chomped, gnashing on the indispensable finger. I could see my own bones. The first one dropped to the floor stuck in the nail-less meat. The second bone crunched into splinters, the third partly gone down the German shepherd's throat and partly hanging straight out from the knuckle joining my hand, surrounded by shredded flesh where a glorious digit had been for so many years so wonderfully attached.

I screamed. I howled. I foamed at the mouth, usurping the dog, I became rabid. I beat my head against the cage and blew my froth in the faces of the men, the public servants. The dog quieted and stared at me with its ears raised. Its teeth were perfectly white, aside from the wash of panted blood. The dog's fat lathered pink tongue hung to the side as it huffed.

The two men pulled me away. The greater part of my finger rested at the German shepherd's feet. I saw the dog pick it up and toss it into the air and catch it back in its mouth, playing with it like a toy. Its teeth closed around it, and I thought the animal swallowed it before the trained killer still playful spit it through a slot in the cage where it fell to the asphalt ground. Dumb with joy, the German shepherd pawed at the gate and whined. It wanted its treat, the vicious innocence of unconscious malice on its face as if it was autistic.

Torture is the refuge of the insecure. One of the officers picked up the remains of my severed finger and put it in his pocket. The other pushed me out of the way. Blood had been spurting from my hand and all over the inside of the van, all over me, and all over them. Sobered, sheepish, and ultimately failed, they got into the van and left. "Better put some ice on that," they said. Regarding my guitar and my finger, they said, "We'll be giving these tokens to Julio when we find him. Consider yourself lucky. And, by the way, if you *are* telling the truth, he lives in Boyle Heights. In case you ever want them back."

I wrapped my hand in my shirt. I did not feel any pain walking half-naked to the emergency room on Sunset Boulevard. The shock was too overwhelming. It iced the pain, yet I was convulsing, on the verge of seizure from scorched nerves. After admittance, though, and before and after surgery, it—the pain—came down on me swift and vengeful, a merciless and vehement, unrelenting panther which has stalked and walked with me in varying degrees ever since, too often greater than the wolf. I have never in my life known such unequivocal distress in any manifestation, physical or otherwise. If I would have known what the psychos were getting at I would have sacrificed the pinkie of my picking hand to the dog.

Who else but I could have such incredibly small hands now? Trickster is the true nature of the gut, more often than not an agent of good but never to be wholeheartedly trusted. For the gut is human: Mischievousness and uncertainty can be found lurking in its wild heart. It is easy to say that I should've never stopped touring, or picked a different city, or quit playing shows with Julio sooner, or even tried better to lie to the cops. But hindsight in my situation is useless. As for foresight, I'll leave projection to God. Authentic prescience is not the dominion of humankind. The sacred but fallible gut regarded with question-able faith is all I had to work with.

Knuckle-fucked and recuperating, if you can truly call it that, I spent much of my time working out blame. Pinning it on Sweet Julio, especially on the girl who worked at the club, and in lesser moments, yes, God—of whom until the dream I was otherwise ambivalent. But none of them were to blame. The ticket woman, Judy, was just trying to do what she thought was right, just trying to help. She and I had slept together a few times. She was a simple and lovely lover, a simple and lovely woman with the best intentions. Unknown consequence is the imperceptible harlot of the decision-maker. The only people to blame were the two cocksucking policemen who likely drifted easily and anonymously back into their professions, into their games, justice void. I filed one report but nothing came of it,

74

despite my testimony of K-9 Unit involvement. Not long after, I slipped away.

A few weeks after I moved into The Amigo, "Sweet" Julio Francisco Villalobos turned up in the obituary section of the *Los Angeles Times.* It looked to be an overdose, but official cause of death had not yet been determined, or released, at press time. The *LA Weekly* did a cover story on their haunted hometown hero while my story went underground. A benefit concert was held in Julio's honor, but I stayed far away from there. Directly or indirectly, it appeared that two of America's finest guitarists had been senselessly murdered. Youth, freedom, sound, the guns gone to the city of dogs.

There are about a hundred nerve endings in the tip of a finger, and I would come to miss every fucking one of them. A worse brunt than if with a normal severed finger because every single one of the glorious microscopic bastards was wired hot and succulent with song.

Then silenced.

In fact, I would come to know the remaining fingers less.

# Chapter Six

FURTHER up the 1, I stopped for a piss and a coffee. And for oil. One day, gone. Getting back into the car, I rolled my pant leg up and fingered the faint scars. After so many years they looked like flat albino raisins where moles had been burned off. I'd kept the wolf from Hal even though it struck a chord with losing the finger: the mythical yang to my harsher canine yin. One had given my song a name; the other had taken it away. Still, it was not so simple. The two histories despite their resonance remained for me irreconcilable. Hal was obsessed with Michigan, and as much as I had come to like the man and confessed to him more of myself than I had to anybody in a long time, I'd at the same time become an expert isolationist and found it necessary to exist privately to a degree and on the periphery of some of Hal's fixations. God and guns I could handle, but Michigan and drugs hit too close to home.

Nostalgia be damned, there was a feeling of nakedness riding with me: My mother embroidered the wolf on the wool blanket as a survival badge of sorts, and now it was gone. After moving into The Amigo I added the geese to it while doing physical therapy on the hand. Pinching and pulling with the remaining appendages is essential in ridding oneself of phantom limbs. Needlework was a decent exercise, masculinity be damned (I was emasculated by losing the guitar, which is ironic because of course the guitar is equally a part phallic and part vaginal machine). My mother's work was elegant, the craft of a toned hand and goodwill. The glory of the wolf jumped from the stitching, its eyes captured alive. My geese were disturbed. They were twisted into scratchy stick figures biting at the sun with one foot in hell, screaming. A death trip of unbounded fury.

Laboring up the coast, nothing but the blatant, unequaled grandeur of California seaboard all the way to the winding redwood corridors of Big Sur, perfectly alone but for that magnificence and the shadow of God following me through the snaking curves of road, I felt a more severe guilt well up inside of me, a face-first collision with my general sense of purposelessness. I felt I did the right thing by taking Hal out of The Amigo for interment, yet I remained in some sense unfulfilled. Selfishly so. I was not looking for any kind of transcendence or validation by burying my friend, but in retrospect it seemed as though I should feel *something*, especially after years of living in indifference. Nothing can replace the finger. But time, which I had wasted so much of, was fast becoming of grave importance as the dream haunted me onward. Was I becoming a believer? Whether it was God or the temptation of legacy burning quietly like a hidden pilot light cloaked by the layers of lassitude inside of me, I suddenly felt de rigueur.

One crippled hand on the wheel, I withdrew Hal's finger bones and laid them on the dash. Then I took out the unfinished letter. Unfolding it with my teeth, I set it on the passenger seat. I glanced at it every few minutes. It had to reveal something I had not seen before. This went on for an hour but on the surface: nothing. On the page it said in ink all that

77

it could. With the ocean crashing along the rocky shore, its spray washing with salt the constructions of epochs spent, Hal washed over me like a cold vapor and I too felt ancient. Turning the letter over, I realized that even in defeat Hal had never once lived his life without immersion.

Then something strange happened. Clarity. It came burning bright under the yellow morning sun: It occurred to me that I had always, erroneously, considered Hal strictly a victim—like me, like I was supposed to be—and that it was the sole reason our spirits were kindred. But taken apart from his anguish, Hal was a victim-cum-victimizer at the mercy of his own tyrant heart—and that too, above all, as I now understood, was the crucial crux where our camaraderie met and dissolved into necessity: prey and predator of unique but somehow equal losses looking to vindicate one another in a world gone haywire with bad connections. One good connection is all it could've taken for love and music and God to come to be. Hal was an outlaw, and I, well, perhaps I was indeed just a pussy. At least in Hal's knowledge of me, post-guitar. Before, I was tough. Blues tough. They say outlaws fuck the hell out of pussies, in so many ways. Who're they? Beyond blood, Hal and I were family by necessity. Maybe we almost succeeded. But not quite. Not yet, I felt, anyway. He'd told it straight to my face and I was too caught up in playing the puppet of melancholia—the clandestine master—to truly see all of the implications in it.

"You got to roll the stone, boy."

"You're one to talk."

"Pardon?" Hal said.

"Pam," I said. "It's enough to make a grown man cry, the way she adores you. You could straighten her out, instead of chasing ghosts. She could straighten you out. You could straighten out each other."

"Watch your mouth, boy. A ghost," Hal scowled. "Nothing

plural, there's only one."

"Well, she's something special. Pam."

"Yeah, she's sweet, but she's too much honey. All sweetness. And I ain't no bear."

We were sitting in his room, the city swallowed up into the night, and it was cold and raining. It was winter in Angeltown.

"I'm just saying," I said.

"When the night falls, all I got is unhappiness," Hal said. "And devotion. That's the key. Remember that. Devotion. Undeniable truth. In the sun, all I really got is unhappiness, the devotion dries. Like old weeds. But the night brings it back to life. Sun is the killer. Night, the giver. You think that's pathetic?"

I didn't say anything. I touched my beard.

"I am man enough to admit it. It's stupid because it ain't ever gonna happen, I'll never have her. She'll never be mine again. I know that. Could I have kept her? Who knows now, but I didn't. I did not keep her, or even try, even though I loved her more than any other thing. You cannot keep what you do not own. But I still believe in it, see? I believe in myself, I believe in that love, because it has not yet died. I know what I am, what I want, everything I want. I believe in honesty. I go to bed with my regret, and I wake doubled with sweat. The sweat of philosophy. Routine, now. Peace?—shit. I know my ride, I been on it long enough. My ride's sole destination is disaster, but I'll take it. So long as I live, nobody gonna take away my devotion. Not you, not anybody. Not Little Pam. Not God." He dabbed his forehead with his handkerchief, no doubt having had taken a plunge before our get-together. "Her name was Maggie. I met her before you were born. She was mine. Together, we made the world. We tried to make the world. We got close."

Hal and I each rolled the whiskey in our glasses.

"At least you tried," I said.

"You don't know shit. The guitar ain't no woman, boy. You

don't know. The problem with you is you only know women as romanticized in song. But me, fuck music. There is no music, there is only she. She was the only music. Now, I'm just this island, unsigned in the final sea. I'll take it, if it remains the truth. That's Truth, capital T. So long as it does, I'll take it. Isolation, the rollercoaster is over. Then again, shit, it begins all over, every day. To hell with the sun. The more night there is, the closer I'll get to where I'm going."

I had heard Hal preach about love many times. His love. About the intricacies of his devotion, about the Greeks. But this was the only time he spoke her name.

"Maggie," I said, as if I were meeting her there in person for the first time. "Hal, Southern California might not be the best place to be if you're an enemy of the sun."

"I live to hate it: sunshine, gas, cola, rock music, happy fucks. The stone, boy. The stone. Sisyphus, yeah. Well, that's us. Eternal frustration for our crimes. Sisyphus knew passion, he knew the uncontrollable nature of the human heart: covet despite consequence. He considered himself a peer of the Gods, the fool. But no more a fool than you or I, we now know, yes we do. We're paying the price for our sins. It's exquisite really, if you can step back and really get a good look at it: the ultimate test of passions. Never turn back and you win, no matter how much you fail. And don't look down, you can look back—you can't go back, but you can look, goddamnit, but not down. Keep pushing, I tell you. You don't even have to move. The stone is your skull, your brain. The Devil himself can't even lick the empty punch bowl of desire so long as you got the guts to ride it out. Even if Sisy's got us beat, we're tragic enough. Greek heroes, you and me."

"Crimes. Not me," I said. "I committed no crime. I did not ask for this."

"Crime," Hal muttered. Drops of rain beat the cracked window in seditious black thumps, erratic rhythms without lightning, without thunder.

"I'm saying that my loss has nothing to do with my passion except that it iced it out of existence." I pointed the nub of my finger at Hal and wiggled it.

"You ain't finished yet. You're just waiting to get royally fucked. Then you'll understand. You give up too easy. I once saw an armless, bucktoothed, and retarded hillbilly in Arkansas play the banjo with his feet. You ought to be ashamed."

"Whatever," I said, waving him off. "I once read about a Spanish eunuch who impregnated a French bull dyke. Immaculate."

"You watch your mouth, kid."

"I'm just saying—"

"Have you ever been in love? I mean real love, the kind of love that feels so good and bad at the same time that you just want to punch yourself in the face forever?"

"Well, I was in love—"

"Don't tell me about the fucking guitar. That's passion, sure. But that ain't love, kid. Real love is scary."

"That's where you and I disagree," I said. "And I wasn't going to talk about the guitar." I poured Hal and I each a lowball of whiskey from a bottle I had brought from my place. Drinking it, I shifted in my hard seat, feeling but squelching the urge to pace about. "But, since you're so apt to attack, if it weren't love, do you think I'd be sitting here with your crusty old ass? And, yes, I have been in love, your kind of love. There have been women. It just never worked out in the end. Maybe a year or two and all the overwhelming excitement, the hot holy red passion, it just flickers out."

"I am talking about *a* woman. Not women. You understand? A woman, one woman. You ever had one of those?"

"Sure, I already told you. And it didn't work out." I was being honest. In all of my years of rambling there were in fact a few women whom I admired so much that the idea of them

81

followed me far beyond our infrequent trysts and I tried with strenuous effort to find home in each. At the same time, no, I had never loved a woman as Hal had loved a woman. There was only the guitar, a species I could unconditionally understand, and that could understand me. Perhaps if I could find a woman shaped like a guitar, one that sounded like a guitar, one that I could play like a guitar, I would love her forever. "No. Hal. Probably not, I guess. Sure, I have loved women, and there are a few I still think about to this day, but I guess they weren't enough or I would have given myself up." The truth is I did think of them, but not enough to actually do something about it. They, along with everything else in my life as I had known it, had been bit into little unsalvageable pieces. I felt incomplete, an echo of myself without reverb—not to be consciously hollered back into the world or even one hell of any woman's longing life. "Or maybe I was always scared. Maybe I am scared still. I don't know. I just played, that's all. I did not pay equal attention to much else. It all seems too late now."

"You're too much in love with an idea of yourself."

"Where's that put you then?"

"You don't know a goddamn thing about my kind of love," Hal said.

"I make a poor Greek," I said.

"A shit hero," Hal said.

Quiet, then he continued:

"Sisyphus is the sun disc. You know that? The personification of it rising and setting. He sinks in the West. How do you feel about that? Here we are. Also, in some circles, he's the sign of the sea, of the treacherousness of the sea, of waves rising, swelling and rising, only to crash over and over and over. At the breaking point. There's no end to it, to him. There's no end to us. We've taken the fall." Hal paused and rubbed his own superb index finger, folding it down into his palm and regarding it as if it were mine, gone. "Whether we asked for it

82

or not."

"I thought you hated the sun," I said.

"I love it enough to know how to hate it. We are one and the same."

Hal drained his glass and I poured two more. When I wasn't out walking or driving I spent most of my days at The Amigo whiskey-drunk from midnight to six, squandering time and expanding my liver. Again, I said her name, "Maggie." Then I said, "Magpie."

Hal's eyes shrunk into infinitesimal black slits. He coiled in his chair, a rattler ready to strike. I slid my chair back a foot, rolled my whiskey around in my glass. The room had grown tense, a bruised lung filling out. I stuck the nub of the finger into my whiskey, put it to my lips, and sucked it. I ran three fingers and one thumb through my beard. Hal let out a great breath, the stressed organ collapsing all around us. The room grew colder. The rain beat harder. The sound of wind on the other side of the pane.

"Shave that godforsaken thing," Hal said.

"Nothing doing," I said. I poured myself more whiskey, ignoring Hal's glass. I said, "You don't know a damn thing about the guitar. That's all I'm going to say about it."

Another wave of tension rose and then broke all around us. Hal again sighed.

"On her old man's farm," he finally said. "We courted, for a long time. Since before I dropped out of high school to work the boats and the light in South Haven. It was a thirty-minute ride between the farm in Bloomingdale and Lake Michigan. After a few years her father accepted my proposal, and I moved in on the farm, in a sort of bride service. So I was working the boats, leaving before dawn and not getting back to the farm until late afternoon, then harvesting well into the dark. No more lighthouse. No more home there. We, my mother and my brother and I, lived up the road. My mother was crazy as a loon.

My father bit it in Korea. After, she just wasn't there in the head anymore. My brother was a beautiful gimp, dashing, a real slick James Dean type, but he'd had his hand mutilated into a sort of crab claw when he got it stuck in a machine while working under the table at a tool and dye plant when he was fifteen. He looked a lot like me, enough to know without question that we were close kin, except he was damn handsomer.

"Well, he'd help out sometimes on Maggie's pa's farm. He couldn't do much, but our kin had become their kin, and vice versa, especially since Maggie and I were going to do the deed. They couldn't stand each other, Maggie and Cyrus, my brother. But Maggie cared for him deeply all the same, like a mother almost, and she felt sorry for him, even though they fought like true siblings. Cyrus could've run any doe down had he not had that mutant claw. It was sad. The women back then could not find their peace with the handicap unless they were real ugly. Only because of their fathers' say. Because the gals, well, they were aware of their panties. But Cyrus couldn't get a wife. The boy was cursed with that fucking thing. That claw. It was a curse on us all.

"Maggie and I were married on a wonderful May Sunday. We moved into the back house on the farm, tried for a long time to make a baby. We never did make one. It was hard on us, not having children. We saw a doctor once, twice, but nothing came of it. But we were in love, so much, Lord knows. Everything else went on about the same on the farm. I have never loved anything of this world like I loved that woman." Hal's eyes shifted to me then back to the floor. "Like I love that woman. For six years we tried to make a baby. We were married six years." His eyes were dry as bleached bones, but everything else about him said he was weeping quietly with terror.

"Well," he continued, "I come home one day and the farm was like a ghost town. I was a little early coming back but not much, maybe half an hour, if that. The lake was too choppy for the dandies who hired the charter that day. Maggie's sister, Clara Belle—over nine months pregnant and her husband run off to Kalamazoo—was having her baby and it was bad, I would find out soon enough, so bad that ma and pa and the midwife had to drive her over to the Allegan Health Center fifteen miles north because the kid was coming out sideways. It didn't seem like anybody was around. I went out to the barn to get a start on the evening haul, and it was there I found them, behind the John Deere on a ratty old oil-slicked raincover, humping.

"I watched them for a few minutes. It was very strange. It wasn't right. I mean aside from ethics. My brother was awkward as hell, pumping like a rusty piston, graceless, jamming into Margaret with the refinement of a bale hook. His claw was raised above him, a flag of pity, snapping in the air like a toothless crocodile, scaly and beastly and revolting. Maggie lay there almost artless. Cyrus was grunting, mumbling stuff at her face, 'Like this? Like this?' Spittle coming right out his mouth and onto hers. Maggie simply lay there, the look on her face was neither of fear nor pleasure in the least. She was indifferent it seemed, at an odd peace. Resignation. Something.

"I went into the connubial house where Maggie and I stayed, and I returned to the barn with my shotgun. I waited until they were finished. Cyrus collapsed atop Maggie, entirely spent from the effort of fucking my wife. He didn't even pull out. I had never hated my brother before, but I did then, and I have never known hate like it since. I walked up quietly. I did not say a word. I put the barrel up to my brother's head. Before he even had a chance to roll off I put one slug through him, spraying his blood and brains all over Maggie and the tarp, and onto the bales of hay behind them. Maggie slid out from under him, her face blank behind a splatter of red as if she did not recognize me or even know where she was. I had only ever been with one other woman, and I never wanted to be with another. I knew in that moment that it was all over, though. No turning back, nothing to cover the mess of irreversible time. The gun was a slug barrel sawed-off. Double-barreled. One barrel smoking, one slug left. I put the gun up to my chin.

"Maggie said in a curious tone, 'Hal.'

"'Yes', I said.

"'Clara Belle's baby come out sideways. Real bad. Ma and pa, they took her in. To the Allegan Health Center,' she said.

"'That so,' I said. 'Shame.'" Hal folded into his chair like a collapsed tin can in a garbage bin. He continued:

"I love her, Lord, oh Lord. I turned and walked out of the barn. I retched. The sun was high, a low-down nasty summer burn. I stared it down until my corneas pulled to white and I pointed the gun at that bad motherfucker and let the slug go. A gang of laughing crows, blacker than the asshole of God, flew from the oaks lining the drive. I never found out why it happened, the betrayal, so sour. Could pity go such a long way? I don't know why I didn't just shoot myself right then and there but wasted it on the sun. I don't know to this day, assuming that she did, when she divorced me. I just left. I never stopped loving her, but I never went back. If only I hadn't pulled the trigger on Cyrus. Maybe. But I did. I did it, and I did not think twice about it. My only brother, whom I loved. I never found out if Clara Belle's baby made it. The whole family was riding on that baby. That baby was the light. That was about forty years ago." Hal grabbed my bottle of whiskey by the neck and drew a long pull from it. Wiping his mouth on his shoulder, he turned to me, eye to eye, and said, "Real love makes a man impulsive." Then he got up, walked across the room, rummaged through some things and brought out an old black-and-white photo cracked with the ravages of time.

"This is the house. The farm. I don't know why I keep it. Torture myself."

Hal handed me the photo. Two old country houses. Silo. Barn. Sad but hopeful looking. I handed it back to him and drew on the whiskey.

"Wonder if it's still there sometimes," Hal said, then slunk back into his chair. "If she is," he said to himself.

"Which hand was it?" I asked.

"What?"

"Your brother. Which hand had been disfigured?"

"Oh. The right," he said.

I felt relieved. We passed the bottle back and forth, then Hal said, "Kid?"

"Yeah," I said.

"Don't ever shoot your brother."

"I'm an only child," I said.

"Me too," Hal said.

"I don't know what to say, Hal. I'm sorry."

"It's a long walk home," Hal said.

We sat there in silence for quite some time, drinking straight from the bottle. Then I poured myself one and raised it. I said, "To Maggie."

Hal stood up and knocked the glass from my hand in a cold slap broiled in bitterness and love and hurt and hatred. At my lips, the drink poured down my beard and neck and into my shirt. I was lucky not to be cut at the mouth. The tumbler broke into large pieces against the stripped hardwood floor. Hal put his hands around my throat and started to choke me. His fingers dug into my neck, threaded into my beard. He looked with coarse determination for something inside my face. I didn't struggle against his clenching grip. The tighter he drew on me, the more relaxed I became. I didn't even try to breathe. I just closed my eyes and with my good hand reached down for the whiskey bottle. Whatever it was he wanted to see he could not find. Or maybe he did. He let me go. It was the closest I ever felt to Hal. As close as I would feel to him when some time later, to make a different point, he would cut off the index finger of his own right hand. I got up and stepped on a large piece of the broken glass, crushing it beneath my shoe as I went to get another tumbler. Sitting back down, I poured us each a long one. I handed Hal his, and we toasted absolutely nothing.

Going further up the coast would be a lie. Michigan had been in the back of my mind since leaving The Amigo, but I was avoiding it. Michigan for me was legend, and it was something I didn't want to touch. Nevertheless...

I put the letter back in my pocket. All of my money was in an account tied to a credit card, and there was enough. In Big Sur I stopped and bought a road map and some very expensive gasoline. The heart of California, Big Sur. California. Gas, cola, rock music, happy people.

Bear.

And us.

*Do you remember rare moments when a sudden light flashed over yourself, your world, God? when you stood on a mountain-peak, seeing your life as it might have been, as it is? one quick instant, when custom lost its force and every-day usage? when your friend, wife, brother, stood in a new light? your soul was bared, and the grave,—a foretaste of the nakedness of the Judgment-Day?*

*So it came before him, his life, that night.*

—Rebecca Harding Davis, *Life in the Iron Mills*

*Ain't nothing gonna put me on the road but The Blues.*

—Sam 'Lightnin'' Hopkins

TWO

# Chapter One

NORTHERN California is not an easy place to leave. The knotty wilds of thrust crags burped from the Pacific eons ago, rolled east into the San Joaquin and Yosemite valleys and riffed higher into the bigger, badder, wilder Sierra Nevada range—well, it can be the end of the line, unequaled in sheer magnificence. Staring at the road map, Michigan seemed a goddamn eternity away. Scanning it west to east was disorienting, as if I had never known a single fucking mile of any of it. One thing I knew for sure was that I did not want to go to San Francisco. San Francisco is no place to reconcile death, passing through or otherwise. The 120 through Yosemite would not do either; every time I had been there—thrice—I had seen bears, even just along the highway, and any time I see a bear, I see my father. The honored dead: I could only handle one at a time, and presently Hal had my number. Halfway to Carmel I turned the car around and went south, back through Big Sur, and aimed the smoker toward the same San Simeon I'd left behind half a day before.

I decided on the 46 through Paso Robles, the route I had

missed out of Los Angeles. I would travel south to get north. The closer I got to the 46 the more I felt the magnet pulling me further down toward the Queen, but I would hold my ground. I did not stop at Piedras Blancas, but I did slow down. Hal had my respects, for all of eternity as far as I was concerned, and paying them there so soon seemed too damn sentimental. In Hal's life I had always been soft, something I wanted to avoid in his death. When I drove past the elephant seals rolling slovenly like giant maggots after a feast, I pissed into the empty coffee cup and threw it at 40 mph into the wind and sand. I took one of Hal's knuckles off the dash and put it into my mouth and sucked on it like an early subhuman contemplating fire. Its taste was of elusive memory, gray and salty. I gave the whole coast of Piedras Blancas the finger and swore on my life, for what it was worth, that despite miles and God and the end of time, the elephant seals—the bears of the sea—and I would meet again one day.

Cutting over on 46, the Hearst Castle impotent but trying, rising chubby and rich and polished but dead to me out of the morning fog, I spit Hal's knuckle piece against the windshield and caught it back in my hand, rubbed it on my collar and tossed it back on the dash with the other two bones. I hadn't had any whiskey in hours. The marooned oaks, bent as dried witches frozen in sacred acts, dotted the black hills of the mountains breaking from the coast, and grew blacker along the road to Paso Robles. This was Mars. A rural alien world, I was in Martian wine country, miles of the grape cascading over the tolerant brown planet interspersed with reds, purples, and greens banded through the tors. I stopped at a winery and bought four bottles of red to subjugate the longing. There would be enough opportunities in Paso Robles for bourbon, but resting there for a brief moment amid the bonny of this Californian sublimity I devised a goal: Make it across the Mojave alive and you can have a taste in Arizona. Find Maggie and make it out of Michigan alive, and I'll quit whiskey forever. Put God to rest, and I'll pick up the guitar again.

Already I knew I was going to avoid the 15 up through the dry rot of Nevada, the armpit of the West. Arizona and New Mexico felt good, felt right, even if a little out of the way. One thing I did not want to do by any means was go into Texas. Troubadours be damned: Crossing the country with God hot on your trail and hell-bent for leather, Texas was no place to be, whether you were a believer or not.

For God, whatever he or it amounted to, was with me now to be sure, though he hadn't yet outside of the dream shown his face or his hand. I could smell him. I could smell him like I have smelled the desert. The desert has a distinct smell like smoke caught in an old glass bottle, interspersed with bits of flesh dried to a brittle crisp, and lizard scat. And I could smell it up to Big Sur and back. Across the bottom rung of the San Joaquin Valley I smelled it. Along the ocean, I smelled desert. Winding through redwoods: desert. Tangled up in grape country: desert. All these places the antithesis of desert, I smelled desert. I smelled desert in these places because desert was now God's smell. And it was spiced with old fire, flakes of death, and petrified reptilian shit. I had smelled it in the dream and He had come to embody it, and He was following me. He was watching me, as if this was my celebrated summer, unknowing that in my mind celebration had become a bitter pill better left crushed and mixed with dog food. God is all-seeing, but he is not all-knowing. There is no other way to explain his dissatisfaction with his own creation, and no other way to explain my loss or anybody else's.

In between Robles and Bakersfield with unscrewed wine I called Him out. Cursing heaven and concentrated as blazing snow through the hot lowlands of cattle stink, pushing hard past the crowded pastures and murderous chutes at Cowschwitz, through Lost Hills and beyond the place where James Dean

95

died (I thought of Hal's brother, Cyrus; half-mockingly yet too serious, I crossed myself), the Hondo oil-choked and affinely winded and winding through the toxic oil fields of Wasco, the giant steel mantises hammering the dirt in metronomic psychosis, I cursed Him until I caught the 58 and moved toward the Mecca of my dream: the Mojave.

"Here's wine, Lord! And heaven is burning! Hot? I'll drink to that. And truth lies in bodies that rot, that turn in soil by the worms, bodies that rot soul first. Yes! Yes. The soul dies first, then the body. Ha! Who would have thought? You? Hardly, it seems. That's why I got your number. Lord."

I waited for an answer. I was putting on the gloves, lacing up. I wanted God in the ring. What did I now have to lose, except... Nothing came but the whip of the wind through the unrolled windows. The radio had been stolen out of the Hondo three years before, and here was God singing zero but you could smell him as far across the basin as you dared to draw in.

"That's right. The soul dies first. I saw it in his eye, God. I saw it in that one frozen unblinking eyeball: gone before the last breath broke out of the gate. If only I could have thought about this earlier. If I could have risen from my own loathing, dragged Hal out of that place and took him on this same ride. Riding shotgun. Shotgun! And alive. If I hadn't been so weak I would've drug his ass back to Michigan myself, guitar or no guitar. If I'd had half the balls Hal had."

I thought if I'd had half of those same balls, then really where was the guitar, too. Not on the seat. Those balls shirked me still. But I was growing something, driving at least.

Hal and I were so resigned to the ritual of talk that we fooled ourselves into believing there was no other option but to suffer. We had convinced ourselves that we weren't apathetic because we were wise, that grief was wisdom, that loss was a badge, which, it turns out, amounted to bullshit because what we had really done was killed action. Life—God's will? Ha!—

had conspired to rob each of us of the things that make life worth living: desire, grace, purpose, pleasure. But I guess none of these things can exist without trial, treason, decree, frustration. Wisdom in spades after the fold. At least Hal was tough.

"Is that it Lord? Hindsight is your only ace? Motherfucker! You are smart, I'll give you that. We stupidly fall for it every time and call it nature. So you're a card shark, a gambler. Well, you listen to me. I'm going to drive this letter to Michigan. That's right. No tricks. You can put a wager on it, but no aces, you hear me? None 'til I get there. I owe this to Hal. You owe it to him. I am going to drop this letter. You said one week. I got a little over five days left, plenty of time to make the drive." I put the letter in my pants, smuggling it.

There remained nothing from God, just his tang. No answers as I rolled over the Tehachapis and entered The Mojave, the desert eerily vacant even for a desert but full of the smell as I lit toward Barstow. Miles of Joshua trees bled dry and shrugging, no longer pointing toward the Promised Land but with limbs cast only down, bent to the hard dirt and dust below, bent toward hell, as if praying for death because the world had failed us all. God was everywhere in Barstow. Stinking up the desert outpost, out-stinking the desert with desert. I stopped for gas on the edge of town and took a piss behind the rundown station, all cracked paint and ragged seams chewed out by the wind, it too looking as if it wanted nothing more than to be swallowed back into the red earth. When I came back around I noticed on a bulletin board hundreds of pages of missing persons bills tacked up, an awful collage of young faces blazoned with "Last seen in Barstow" pasted above their foreheads. The pages ran ten across by ten high and in some places ten pages deep. Many of them were children. Most of them were women.

And there's supposed to be a living God, I thought. "Well, buddy, if you're going to end it all, whatever which way, it's about time and all too late," I said, and with the desert starting to broil at high noon and stifling my lungs with the scent, I felt cold with the shame of being alive and in the whole pot of humanity having lost only a finger. I shivered at the thought of what happens too often to those who go missing, especially the hunted young and female.

I got into the car, uncorked more wine, and blew toward Arizona.

The first time I ever set foot in Los Angeles was on a howling dry midnight in a cranked mid-'90s trans-American July, akin to the present path, but the reverse. I had ridden the Mojave line across red Arizona on the 10 West—that selfsame mother-fucker of a road that I would flee from L.A. upon—and as the high desert broke in a dusty wave frozen over the delinquent basin of the San Andreas Fault a hundred million lights shim-mered up out of the bruised haze that was sandwiched between the black walls of craggy mountain, and I thought: Memory, memory, memory, I am entering a phantom's world. Somehow it was all familiar. As if my ghost, with me still alive, was already bound to this land. I felt like I was in space floating toward the most peaceful Armageddon only imaginable in an electric guitar future, some terminal intergalactic blood-and-circuit board where all of nature smashes its selves into ingratiating peace. I'd already felt like I was going home. But all of this seemed as a means to a good end, not The End. A break, but not to be broken.

I was mesmerized and drawn to California as if toward some-thing that could surely kill me, like the wolf—like a bear—but only to make me more alive, like legend, and I trusted it. I'd never once thought about the possibility of losing a finger, a hand. I could not help but follow the awakening serpent all the way to its palpitating heart: Our Lady, the Queen of the Angels. I'd remained fully hypnotized by the tranquil hum of the lights rolling in a neon tongue swathed in browns and greens between the Cajon Pass and the biggest living thing on Earth: the Pacific Ocean. I was on tour then, entering into California for the first time. As the glittering spectacle sharpened past Redlands, beyond the listless streets of San Berdoo and another hour-plus haul through the fluorescent pike of the San Gabriel Valley, I finally made out the skyline of Angeltown materializing from the fog and outer space. I remember the monument of it all quickly shedding its outskirts as greater Southern California shifted into a feudal haze. I had pierced myself into the racing *Corazón*. L.A. resonated for me a strange intimacy. I had always known her even though I had yet set foot to her, an ethereal magnet tailored for my own wanting endorphins, like the sweet pink lobes of a Venus Flytrap luring its prey, or the way first sex with someone you've so longed for feels like a new world has opened yet somehow part of you, no matter how fantastic it all is, knew how it would be all along.

On the road to Michigan, though I had just gotten on the 40 and was avoiding the 10, I was fighting the old echoes as I crossed into Arizona west to east. With bloated wino tripe eyes, starving for and from California and Hal and God, I prayed to make a town where whiskey flowed for currency before the apex of the sun cracked its white fangs across the back of my neck. Fearing to be bled as dry as the two empties of red wine beneath the seat. I was leaving California for the first time in six years, and it hurt. Yes, Los Angeles is the pimp mime of smiling daggers and winsome decay, and pray-tell I would live long enough to return. Losing the finger there made it the nucleus of pain, and in order to be whole again—I was quickly and vastly learning as foreignness transgressed into pugnacious reality; as I left the bear in the rearview mirror—to that nucleus, that old heart pumped full of angst, I must one day return. The trouble was that time seemed to be God's ante alone.

But for now? I only needed whiskey. Screwing the town of

Yucca, too of name for the auspices of my cardinal shadow, and sure enough smelling like it, slowing down into Kingman, Arizona, twenty-five more miles toward the end of the desert, I scanned the horizon for a tavern or a liquor store, and for the first time I heard God laugh.

# Chapter Two

SOME thirty hours later I crossed the Michigan state line. It was blood black/red dusk collapsing into night, and the stars were already out. The air smelled of the sweet funk of ready fruit. No wind and the endless sound of crickets. It was midnight when I crossed the Van Buren County line. Thick woods woven through miles and miles of rolling yellow and green fields made blue by the planter's moon. Great oaks, pines, maples, elms. Rows and rows of corn, cherries, blueberries, apples. This was, as they say—even those who have yet to meet him—God's Country. All the more to fear it because they are right. I could feel Him ubiquitous, the entire Midwest reeking of the empire of dust no matter how full of life it was. Out of the Southwest the smell remained and even seemed to grow stronger the further away. Mountains, plains, forests: God remained. A barbarian stalking the perfect night sky, death's bright angel of His own design, embouchure tight as ass, blowing perhaps with our very shotgun a Gabriel's Horn of terrible oppression. My pores opened like spiked veins. It does not cool at night in the summer in Michigan. The humidity does not wane. The sweat rolled out of my body fuming with life. This place was Hal incarnate: hot and green and worked, melancholic and beautiful, damned but full of glory all the same, Michigan. I had not slept in two days. I had not dreamt since the dream. I had driven 2,658 miles in less than 50 hours. Gas and oil and drink. Almost straight through, except for one breakdown in Nebraska.

My hands trembled as I wheeled through the languorous Michigan country roads, brain burned, no longer knowing if I needed more or less whiskey and coffee to survive. My heart was out of tune, raging in 33/4 time. I hadn't eaten a thing, and I was shaky. The last food I had seen was Little Pam's chicken. I should have died three times over of alcohol poisoning, but the adrenalin kept me going. The heart is a wonderful and stubborn beast. The great northern lights raking in the cosmos flashed kaleidoscopic disjointed rhythms through the canopy of branches above. In the open roads skirting endless fields, it seemed there was nothing but the determined heat of the estival night slapping like a demon's balls onto the dusty ass of the Hondo. I was weak and I was lost.

Hal had once told me that Van Buren County has more fruit acreage than any other county in Michigan. It was true. Along County Road 388 I eased the Hondo into a bowled ditch alongside a giant farm, got out, wandered into the bountiful plot, and gorged on sweet, dark cherries until my tight gut grew forth and shrugged over the top of my belt. I cracked my teeth repeatedly on pits like chewing rocks, swallowing some of them. I hoped a pit would grow a tree in my stomach, a thick, fruitful son of a bitch to break my throat and toss my skull like a seed. It was the greatest thing I have ever tasted.

Wandering through the labyrinth of farm, the sticky juice and bits drying in my beard, I found a small grove of peaches on which I too gorged and gorged until I could barely walk. I spent costly hours in the orchards drunk to exhaustion on the fruit.

Blood sugar getting high enough to turn an elephant diabetic. Then I found apples. Hastily I plucked one and bit hard into foul, foul bitterness. It was too early. The cherries and peaches were ripened to perfection, July harvesters, but the apples weren't ready. The old garden would not fall on this day. My throat burned and my jaw imploded, and, the acid rising in my stomach after so much indulgence following so much neglect, I fell to my knees and belched a stream of tangy blood orange-colored vomit onto the orchard path. Fruity bits and blood, about a half-pint of blood. I'd been peeling back my stomach lining with alcohol for so long that my digestion had turned ulcerous. I wiped my mouth, my beard on the grass, and my hands, too, after catching some of it only by accident. I don't know how long I sat glutted in the field, but dawn was coming. I moved to get back on the road, but when I rose to turn for the Hondo I found a large man in overalls looking down on me with an acute concern etched into his face. It seemed he'd been in this predicament before. In his hands: ever my hunter, my temptress. It had been exactly 2,902 miles since I had left Los Angeles, and, as if I'd been driving in circles, here was another shotgun offered to my face.

I looked to the sky and waited for the sound, but it did not come.

HAMEN.
    HA MEN!
    Was the snigger.
    God's laugh.
    Chilling enough for me to forsake him and whiskey for the rest of Arizona, on up ghostly New Mexico, all through the night banked against the continental spine and the dry lowlands of eastern Colorado, and into blood country: Nebraska. Though I wanted whiskey more than anything—the Hondo was good so long as she had oil, but the grain had become my fuel—I left

Kingman and all three states from there to Ogallala dry as virtue. Partly because I was nearly shocked to death by his manifest HAMEN!—Ha! Men, you self-righteous bastard!—ringing my spine and sending tremors through the fiery caloric air, and, steadying myself, also because I needed to prove some strength, some ground. If I'd shown God this soon in our game that I had no discipline, then I might as well have lit my own self on fire, or crawled toward him begging for the barrel as a baby for the tit.

Just out of Ogallala, Nebraska, I stopped to finish Hal's letter. A roadside tavern called Score's. Full of third-shift factory workers just getting off, their night beginning as the sun breaks over the eastern horizon. All-American ghouls by trade doing their best to get by. The backbone of the nation, and they were rowdy, hard gruffs reconciling with the agony of existence the best way they knew how: beer and brotherhood. I ordered three whiskeys and found a dark corner.

One in—here's to you, Lord, I made three states without it, sucker—my nerves downshifting, I withdrew it. The words were wrung with longing. It was hard to look at them without tearing up. Just two words: "Dear Magg," the saddest poem on Earth. Hauntingly beautiful—frightening, really, as so many truly beautiful things are. It was like a religious artifact, and I was like a believer. I had felt so far that it needed to be finished, but now it seemed so complete I did not know what to say. Pledging allegiance to it, I drank the other whiskeys and ordered more. The paper it was written on was yellowed, almost brittle, and sitting there staring at it for however long over however many whiskeys, it occurred to me that it was a blank leaf page torn out of the back of an old hardcover book. It was just the right size. I brought it to my nose. I could smell it. It had that smell, the unmistakable musk of printed libretto soaked in time. I hadn't brought any of Hal's books with me. Sitting in that sticky, smoky bar on the edge of the Old West while burned-out line-punchers alternated between singing union songs and gazing me down with disconcerted red eyes, I felt the urgent need to turn around and drive back to L.A. for the sole reason of finding out which book Hal had intended to finish.

"Who was she?"

"Huh?"

One of the gruffs broke from the group, caught me sniffing the paper. "Letter from someone who ain't around no more, eh no?"

"Ah. Sort of," I said.

"Whatcha drinkin'?" He was covered in crusted denim and had a long handlebar mustache which he twirled to points with the beer caught from his pint.

"Whiskey, mostly."

He went to the bar and came back with two beers, two whiskeys.

"Thanks," I said.

"Payday."

"Well, here's to that," and I raised one to him.

"You passing through west or passing through east?"

"I'm not sure anymore," I said.

He looked at me for a sour second, then he said, "East. You from the West."

"How can you tell?"

"Just can. You's eyes crazy enough. If it'er the other way, wouldn't've boughten you one."

I filled with a smug elation. I had graduated something, passed a test I hadn't known I'd taken, the exam which had yet to have a name, or perhaps even a purpose. Not that I have ever been ashamed of being from the Midwest, or from Chicago, a true city of The Blues—far from it, a sanctified pride all its own. But embodying the West in that moment made me feel as if I had earned the right to leave it behind and I felt a rush of fear run out of me and into the cracks of worn linoleum below.

I looked down at the missing finger. My finger on my fret hand. The bill had been paid.

"To the West," I said, and I raised my glass.

"My friends, my crew back over at the bar, they think you's a bum faggot lost and scared, 'cept they thrown about the beard. That thing make you look crazy. Either way, they put it stiff to their skulls that you a stone fool. Maybe even a pervert. They'd liken to kick your ass if they get drunk enough. It is payday, after all. But I know how it is. I'll hold them off. My old lady used to leave me notes like that, all drenched in perfume. That was a long time ago. She gone now."

"Oh, this," I said, fumbling the letter.

"I carried those letters with me 'til they crumbled into dust. Tortured myself." He took a long plug of his beer and sucked the foam loudly out of his mustache without fingering the ends. "You runnin' from her, or runnin' toward her?"

"Both, I guess."

"I hear you." He leaned in close, reeking of grease and sweaty testicles and with breath stinking with the acid of old crimes and new acquiescence into quiet doom. "Hey buddy, can you do me a favor?"

"What's that?"

He looked over his shoulders to see if his pals were watching. Even though nobody was looking just then he still gave them the bird. "Could you..."

I waited.

"Could you let me smell it?"

"Man," I said. "I don't know."

"I understand."

The longing in his tired face was too much. "Okay."

I lifted the letter to his nose. He breathed deep. His eyes closed to some far away place that once existed so real that it had likely ruined all other places in time that followed. He held it for a long time, relishing it, as if he actually could smell the fragrance he so desired. Then his face crinkled into an angry purple raisin. "Shit, man. That don't smell like nothing but an old moldy fuckin' romance novel, man! Get that shit outta my face."

"It's old perfume. Older than music. Maybe even older than death."

"You are crazy."

"Crazy as time," I said.

"Fu-uck."

"Brave with love, so goes down the Devil," I said.

He left disgusted, walked right out of the place and did not come back. I drank my whiskey and beer, and his, too. I went back up to the bar, asked for a pen, two more whiskeys. One for me, one for Hal. Nobody bothered me. I finished the letter.

I got back in the Hondo, onward east, before any other chance of the bar hounds getting too frothy. I pushed her hard, got her up to ninety, high and satisfied and determined—even fearless—feeling drunk with balls the size of steeple bells, when through the funnel of dawn there He was, a deer in my headlights. Standing in the middle of the fucking road like a transient ghost: God. Dressed in blue jeans and cowboy shirt, a wheat shoot between his teeth, with the same cricked wooden face and cracked leather smile as the old loner in the dream. I slammed on the brakes just shy of blowing through him and cut fast into tight circles, spinning across the empty highway and through barbed fencing and into a steaming cattle field beyond. Twisters of smoke trailed after in consequential goblins. For a moment I could not tell if I was in one piece, if the car had rolled, if The Man had indeed come around. If He had taken me before it was time. I sat frozen to the back of the seat, my knuckles burned white to the steering wheel, save for the solo nub sticking straight up and trembling back and forth in a volt-ammeter of complete fear. Though it was high summer in the Great Plains, the ascending aorta of blood country, I could see

107

my breath bouncing off the windshield in short puffs. My heart was wedged up in my throat. I scanned the highway, but the phantom was gone. Instead, the road was growling with speed. Traffic that wasn't there thirty seconds before blew across it as if dropped by a tornado, and none of them noticed me.

I got out of the car, shaky and sobered. Eight, ten whiskeys, wasted. I walked around the Hondo, one foot on grass, the other ankle-deep in manure. The right rear tire was blown. I walked back up to the edge of the highway. No sign of God, no laugh this time.

"That's because this is not funny," I howled. "I could have died. You gave me a week."

The voice of gravel came: "Still can."

"Still can what? Have my week?"

"Die."

I contracted my eyes deep into the horizon looking for the source. I did not look up because if there was a heaven I did not want any part of it. I kept my eyes burrowed into the single spot in the road where we'd almost collided. It was empty. Emptiness interrupted every few seconds by the streak of someone doing ninety on their own road to salvation.

When I got back to the car I searched around the floor-boards and found Hal's knucklebones. I put them back on the dash before rolling up my sleeves and my pant legs. Knee-deep in cow shit, I put on the donut. The trunk was situated around Hal's ghost, the invisible J cleaved into it as an anchor would. I had to dig pounds of dung out from beneath the wheel and then gather stones from the highway embankment in order to raise the jack high enough out of the slough to get the job done. Strained bovine yowls cracked afar in the dew. A handful of cows walked up and watched me from a comfortable distance. They were smiling.

Rearranging the trunk to accommodate the wheel without disturbing Hal's ghost, I found his gun. It glowed like a vigilante, compromised and angry. The barrels were sawed down and the handle was shortened, the stock honed as if it were a handgun. I took it into my hands, tracing its lines, afraid and comforted by its icy stillness. I hadn't checked the chambers. I did not check them now. I raised it up in my right hand, the three fingers and one thumb of my left hand dancing a song against my thigh.

"Good Lord!" I said.

I said: "Hey, God!"

I said: "I got my own."

And with that, I did look for heaven. And when I found it I unhitched the safety and pulled the trigger, sending one solid ballistic projectile hungry for it burning through space. I waited for the report.

"HAMEN!" He snorted. Just once, without hurt, without pity. The clouds over Nebraska were zoomorphic cumulus in the shape of trampling animals coming down: elephant seals. Then all was quiet. Perfect blue. Not even the sad moan of the old Bessies off swollen with milk.

I must have missed.

I put the safety back on and put the gun back in the trunk. I had to rock the Hondo about sixty times to get it out of the dung pit. I was lucky not to have ground the transmission out. I rode that goddamn donut at ninety all the way to Omaha before getting a real replacement tire, daring anything to get in my way, thirsty and angry, sailing past the halfway mark, driving for Michigan. Watching the West close like a giant exhausted bloodshot eyeball in the rearview mirror.

"You're not God," I said, plucking spew from in between my fingers, the orchard spinning all around me.

The man was the size of an oak wine barrel on stilts. His gun was a pump action single barrel. He smiled down on me with black teeth rotted into little corn niblets. "God, son? Hell no. I'm be a demon, you don't start explaining."

Fried, every atom of my body was nerves. "You got slugs in that or buckshot?"

"Rock salt and nails, to tell the truth. But it will do the trick."

"That's not what God said," I said.

"Are you drunk? What is this about God? You drunk?"

"I wish. Sir. I was. I mean, I was drunk. Before. Wish I still was."

"You a coyote?"

"Coyote?"

"Brigand."

"Coyote, no. But I am from the West."

"I say you are," he said.

I reached into my pocket and pulled out my wallet. I took out what cash I had, about thirty bucks. From my shirt pocket I retrieved the photo. "I'm not a thief. I'm sorry. I'm lost. I hadn't eaten in days." I held out the picture. "I need to get to this place. It's a...it's a family emergency. I've been running so hard I've forgotten to eat. All the way from California."

"Californeea." He spat a thick stream of yellow juice from between his black teeth. He took the photo but kept the gun trained on me. Holding the old black-and-white photograph between his pinkie and ring finger, he removed a pair of taped-up bifocals from his bib overalls. I looked at his hands. They were thick with calluses. He had all of his fingers. "Bad enough the coyotes come, tear up our barn cats and put the hounds to test, not to mention what few goats I got. You're the first talking one I've ever seen."

"I'm no coyote," I said. Though maybe I was. I was some breed of canine. In the land of dogs how could one roam otherwise. "I'm a wolf," I said. I held out the money.

"Wolf? Pfff. That's even worse." He put on his glasses and studied the image. "I do believe I know this place. Don't look

110

the same though. You playing straight with me?"

"Yes," I said. I said, "I am only lost." I said, "That fruit of yours, that was the sweetest thing I have ever tasted."

"I may be wrong, but I believe this is the old Conchobhar farm, down CR 380 way, other side of town."

"Bloomingdale? Is it Bloomingdale? How far?"

"Yeah, Bloomingdale. You're close. Just a few more miles east, other side of Great Bear Lake."

"Bear. Lake."

"Yeah. Great Bear Lake. Good fishing."

"You know the farm? Are you sure?" I asked.

"Yeah, only because of the fire."

"Fire?"

"Yeah, the old woman who lives there—if she's still alive—her land went fallow for good after her husband died. She kept the farm, had people work it, but after a time nothing came back. It was strange, we'd have the warmest, nice wet years, and not even a damn ragweed would grow in those fields. I guess she couldn't take it. Didn't have no family, I don't think. Couldn't keep any hands on."

"What about the fire?"

"Yeah. There was two houses on that property, just like this," he held up the photo. "She went into one of them houses one day and just lit it on fire, maybe herself as well. Even the city papers out of Kalamazoo and Grand Rapids came out for that story." He let the shotgun come down.

"Maggie? Ahem. Margaret?"

"What?"

"Was Margaret her name. The woman? Maggie?"

"Don't say I know. Don't recall. Say, though, I thought you said you'in family circumstances." He raised the barrel back up.

"Friend of the family. More of a messenger."

"You come all the way from Californeea jus' to deliver a message? You ain't got no phone?"

111

"It's important," I said. "Gravely."

"I don't know…"

"Please," I said. "I can get you more money if there's a bank in town, an ATM. Bloomingdale. 380, tell me how to get there."

He handed back the photograph, folded up his glasses and put them back in his breast pocket. He took the thirty dollars. He let the shotgun down, rested it against his leg and counted the money. Peeling off a ten and a five, he handed the other half back.

"Judging from your guts over there, this should do on the bill. Why don't you come up to the house and clean yourself up. You stink like fertilizer, too."

"I got stuck in a field of cow shit in Nebraska."

"Well, come on. And don't cuss in front of my wife."

"Thank you," I said, "I can't thank you enough."

"Once is enough," he said.

"Thanks."

He shot a crooked eye at me. "Californeea, Christ. The wife's got some bacon, eggs, grits goin'. You don't puke in my house you can help yourself. Coffee, too."

"Mister—"

"Hawkins."

"Mister Hawkins, I know it's six in the morning, but what I could really use right now is a shot of booze. You can judge me all you want, but I'm all nerves. It's been a rough one. Whiskey, preferably."

"Hawkins is my first name. Clemens is my family name."

"You got any whiskey, Mr. Clemens?"

He stared at me hard one more time. "I do believe so," Hawkins Clemens said, "but not in front of the missus," and then he led me to his house on the other side of the orchard. On a county road in Michigan the merciful angel burned bright.

Californeea. Michigan. Hal. Shotguns. Bear.

Circles.

# Chapter Three

I found the house. Hawkins Clemens was right. It was on CR 380, on the other side of town. Small one-horse Bloomingdale: just a four-way crossroads in the woods. Not even a stop light. Only a bank, market, gas station, post office, school. And a town square decked to the gums with red, white, and blue streamers and U.S. flags, ribbons. Geared up for the Fourth of July celebrations. Three days, a clawing reminder. The place had the ceremonial air of a strong cocktail of patriotism and Christianity. I stopped in the market and to slighted looks bought three fifths of whiskey, a stranger in town. Fodder: I drank a quarter of one fifth in the few miles from town to the farm, calling on my nerves like a hunter on his dogs.

The place was old, a tired old farmhouse with a barn-shaped roof and second-story windows spaced like eyes lived in too long. The land lay ratty—fallow no more, but tangled in weeds as tall as I, the alfalfa and soybeans or whatever once grew there long gone. The farm was as active and fruitful as petrified wood. The ragged wooden white house sat atop it like a headstone. A grain silo choked in gray ivy leaned unsure but semi-erect beyond the small grove of walnut trees at the edge of the fields, an old cock pointing toward the setting sun—pointing west—pushing for one more shot of glory before the bring-down. For the first time since I set foot in Michigan there was a wind. I left the Hondo in the ditch along CR 380, parked at the mouth of what was once a gravel driveway now overgrown with ragweed. Hal's oak trees were gone. Another testimony of a human time and place in the world being swallowed back into the same earth that had borne it for just so long.

I unscrewed the bottle and took three long pulls. The other two fifths were in the trunk with the gun, and I was tempted to simply empty this one, roll up the letter, put it in the bottle, and let it sail into the tall grass and get the fuck out of Michigan before dark. I was scared. The place was crawling with ghosts, and Hal, Hal the young man, younger than I presently was and already Cain, was one of them. Where the old barn must have been was a long, wide pile of ancient rubble. Remnants of cracked beams jutted up out of mounds of broken roof tile and gutted concrete foundation like snapped masts belched from the cantankerous sea. As for the guest house Hal had spoken of, I saw nothing. Hawkins Clemens must have been right about that, too. No trace of it whatsoever, though I was sure that this was the place. The air surrounding the plot was too thick with fervent witness and the ferrous scent of blood and autumn—as if summer only ended here, the air grew dark and spiny in these acres in early July, cool here in an otherwise oven-baked Midwest—to not be it. Besides, I had the photograph: the same piece but once warm with the matrimonial quarters.

I walked up to the house. I stood there staring at the door, wanting her, Maggie, old burnt up Maggie the martyr to come to me, a savior to put her wise hand on my brow like a faith healer and take it all—this holy road I'd been howling on—and make it go away. Welcome the wayward Mercury, O Maggie the Saint, Maggie you who have taken and lost and who have become legend—not for me, not for me goddamnit! But yes, me too!—but for what I've come to know: for a sad old junkie who prayed to you daily—do you remember him? Saint Margaret? Of course you do, but how?—you are the reverse Holy Virgin who will make all of this loss and confusion that is the world become unborn.

I summoned my guts and knocked on the door. Nothing came. I moved to the window on the same side of the house but it was too high. I went around the corner and peeked in. The place was furnished but appeared empty, as if its occupants had one day simply turned to the same dust as that which time is measured by, coating the sills on the other side of the windows shut tight to the cold on this very hot July day. A fine medicine good for spiders and bad for those with lungs. I felt allergic just looking at the stuff, cobwebbed as far into the room as I could see. There was a long couch, two high back chairs, end tables with brass lamps, a short, plump divan, and a grandfather clock. Lurking in the shadows was a specter most unexpected: a piano. I looked at my hands, palm-up, then palm-down. I rattled seven fingers, two thumbs in the air as one would against the ivory, and my throat tightened. I was never any good at the piano. Not good enough, anyway, even though it and the guitar are some-what interchangeable, notes and lines and chords and such, but it stoked the fire nonetheless. Gaping at it as if a jailed conjugal lover separated only by the glass and time, long on patience I ached for it. It was the first time I had the lust without fear to touch a musical instrument since...

I went back around the house to the door to see if it was locked, momentarily divorced of my supreme mission and birthing the desires of another, when I was stopped cold at the foot of the stoop. A woman. Standing there. Flesh, flush, rosy. Not an old woman, not what could have been Maggie. But a young woman. In her kind thirties, if that. Standing on the small concrete block porch in a green summer dress that came just below her knees, her red hair blowing living blood into the harrowed dried stains that saturated the wraithlike prairie. Her face a living sea of freckles, her pink ankles alive and stretched. She stood on her toes, looking at the Hondo and then to me as if she had been expecting somebody else. Her feet were bare, and her legs were long. The dress was armless and her arms were long. She shielded her eyes with her long hands growing long fingers and her high tortured brow seemed to ask, *Why?* The sight of her was, in every sense that the Midwest can so deeply conjure, sad and beautiful.

"I'm sorry to bother you," I said.

She just stared at me.

"I ran out of gas," I lied. I don't know why I did it, but I did it anyway. In the face of God, too. "And I need to use the bathroom."

Quixotic little bird, I thought, when she remained quiet with nothing but incomprehension inscribed into her sweet dreamily disturbed face. Big blue eyes piercing in the wind as if trying in her mind to put something together about some instance that took place a long time ago.

"I could try someplace else, maybe up the road..."

She sat on the stoop and started braiding her hair, the luscious crimson veins circulating through her fingers like living serpents. Nervous and unsure, I turned to go, thinking, Screw Hal and Maggie, and God, and you, Red, and pianos, too, when she belted out an agonizing shrill, a glass-shattering octave sending a dozen ravens into flight from deep within the walnut trees. It lasted for thirty seconds, an eternity. Then she closed her lips and went on with the braids.

"Are you okay?"

She answered me not.

"I lied," I said. "I do not have to use the bathroom. In fact, I pissed over there next to your mailbox after I parked the Hondo, which is in fact full of gas and ready and willing to blow smoke out of here. And I'm getting on a drunk, too."

She started coughing. Coughing, coughing. To no end, thick and miasmatic, the butter in her lungs churning.

"Jesus. I mean, are you all right?"

She screamed again, this time loud enough to shake the walnuts from the trees, grenades of the fruit of the nut bouncing once off the old weed-garroted gravel and then sitting green-split and virginal as the cold wind that grew only here briefly faded. The place turned verdant, alive, but only for a moment, a flashing mirage of old glory. A reprise to her reprise.

"Okay, okay. I'm looking for Maggie. Margaret. Margaret S.—no, Connor, or, uh, uh, Conchobhar, or something, Margaret C., something or other, just Margaret, just Maggie—there is a message, and I...fuck. Pardon me. I. I am the bottle." I looked at the whiskey in my hands and I felt ashamed. I took another drink.

More silence as the silkworms turned and the sun faded and God mixed the dust.

"I said I'm looking for M—"

Like a crow she flew to my stead. She put one hand to my throat. With the other she placed a solitary index against my lips, sensuously shutting me up as if our moment was becoming conspiratorial. Her eyes darted all around. The cold grew colder. The weeds in the field seemed to tower into the sky, obscuring the distance. She held me tight and awaited my reciprocal as two lovers would do to warm each other. Then, with long fingers intertwined with mine, she led me into the house. Spiders clicked in the tomb. No fingers were missing from either of her long prairie hands.

"You should just be grateful you got nine left."

"Don't mess with me. I'm in no mood," I said. It was another midnight at Hal's. I was crying like a baby into the bitter moon, feeling particularly crazy and fervent in convincing myself that life and all there was to it had been chewed off forever.

"And shave that fucking thing," he said.

Hal hated my beard. He thought it made me look too crazy. "Beards are for homeless people and queer intellectuals," he'd say. "Respect your face. For when you finally meet God. You have to be presentable, or he won't take you seriously. How you gonna play on his turf looking like a vagrant gnome? He'll laugh at you. He'll take one look at you and STAMP: *File this poor bastard. Next.* Face, you hear me? That's your ace. That's the shank in your pocket, when you're up against it, going for the big store."

"I'm keeping it until I find the finger." I had grown the beard simply because I didn't care anymore. It was two years long at this point and never trimmed: hostile, wiry, and Irish.

"It's not just God, you know. You have to trick the Devil, too. You gotta look a little crazy, a little clean, enough to make them both insecure. Stubble is fine. Look at me. But total lunacy, come on. They cut that deck. The beard's a giveaway."

It was about six months after he'd told me about the incident on the farm and about a year before I'd had the dream. "To hell with them. I'm not playing their games."

"Ho, shit. You were born playing their games, son. You really are a piece. Just when I think you got a head about you, or at least some balls. I don't know. The only dice you got on that finger is in heaven or hell. You think it's still pickled on ice somewhere in Boyle Heights? That's a fool rub. The dice of God are always loaded."

"I'll find it."

"That goddamn digit is green with death. It's a fuckin' curse on your brain. It's infected, and it's infecting you. It's just a finger. A minor league loss—"

Here it comes—

"You ever kill anybody?"

118

"Yes, Hal. I have. I've killed Sweet Julio for six hundred days straight. I kill him every night. I kill Bug Wallace every time I walk by his goddamn room. I kill dogs in the streets. I kill wild, rabid dogs and I kill primmed dogs crapping on green lawns. I kill service dogs. I kill lovely ticket girls in rock clubs. I kill the police in the darkest alleys of my mind. I killed God and the Devil before they were even a thought in some poor caveman's peanut. I kill you every goddamn time you tell me that my loss is minor league, and I especially kill you when you ask me if I have ever killed anybody."

"I wish. I wish you had the guts. Would've made dragging your ass back here at least interesting. I had hope for you."

"Well I am truly sorry."

"I got thirty years on you, kid. Probably more. You're just playing games here and you don't even know it. And I guarantee you, them games are being gambled on your soul. You think you're helpless. This," he raised his marked arms to heaven, "is helpless."

"Bruises fade."

He was as furious beneath his purple skin as a Gila monster sitting on a desert rock just waiting for the right motherfucker to come along.

"Look, Hal. See, I'm grateful, alright. I'm glad to be alive, even though I feel bad all the goddamn time. But you. You—"

"Me what."

"No, I don't know what it's like. To actually do it. But. You could have gone back, I don't know, tried something. I'm not trying to simplify it. I'm just saying. Maggie wasn't divorced from existence. You left her breathing. You're right. My finger ain't breathing. But your Maggie, she just might still be."

"I did not leave my brother breathing."

"I'm not talking about your brother."

Hal emptied his glass, slammed it down on the armrest. Got up from his chair, walked over to the cedar box, retrieved his goods, and sat back down. He took a wad of brown heroin, dropped it in his spoon, torched it. Dropped in a cotton ball. Hypodermic in the cotton ball, plunger pulled. Tied off with a rubber hose that looked like it came from a child's chemistry set. Tight around his arm as if he were trying to strangle it. Found swift with rough slaps the willing vein. Needle drops. Blood flows out into the rig, mixes with the medicine, and flows back in. Same as it ever was since the first holistic fix: His music begins.

I reached down for the bottle, poured myself one. I drained it. I drained another. No music. I did not refill Hal's glass.

Hal sat collapsed into his chair, the rubber tube dangling. "I should jam this fucking rig right into your eyeball, son. Tell me about loss. Tell me about divorce. Tell me, *me*, about killing. Tell me about God and the Devil and all you're missing is three-quarters of one finger. That, *that*, could be fixed."

It was one of the very few times Hal had used in front of me and the only time it was ever so blatant. He was already high when I walked in. Now he was just trying to make a point.

"You just don't get it. The guitar was my Maggie. Is that so hard for you to understand?"

"Yes. It is. No. Not entirely."

Hal got up and floated to the bathroom. He was gone for a considerable amount of time. I heard the water running in short bursts. I sat with the whiskey, fuming and caged and then exhausted. When he came back he was clean shaven and pouring sweat. Before I even noticed the blood, Hal dropped his severed finger into my lap and sat back down. He grinned, blood screaming from the blunt empty space in his right hand, the thumb sticking straight up and pulsing red, and the middle, ring, and pinkie fingers curled under and totally white. It was the index finger of his right hand. It looked like the mirror of how my hand once looked, unbelievably and forever challenged. Cut clean off with his straight razor.

120

"See. I'll still play," Hal said, and he passed out with a smile on his face, high and just. "I will find a way," on his lips as his eyes went down.

He threw the finger out of the window on the way to the hospital, told the surgeon it was a shaving accident and that the finger went down the drain. When we got back from the hospital, Hal bandaged and numb, with a sack of the same drugs I had spilled on the day we met, and me stuck with the bill, I said one thing to him: A right finger is not a left finger, but nice try.

"I'm right handed. It'll be harder to shoot. But I'll learn with the left."

"It is not the same, Hal."

"I'll tell you what. You go out and get a guitar, make do with it. You do that, and I'll go back to Michigan. See about her."

"We'll see," I say.

"No see. Only do. Or no deal."

Hal was of course right. I should have done. We should have done. The guitar was my Maggie, not heroin, and Hal never made it back to Michigan. He played, but then again no he did not.

I find myself inside the house. Hawkins Clemens is right. This is it.

The inside of the house is dead. All sad stillness, a crypt of quiet oblivion. There are no pictures on the walls. The dust coats everything, every room. Red, the girl, leads me upstairs. She cuts through cobwebs with her straight fingers. Lining the staircase are faded shades beneath the dust where picture frames once hung. We pass one closed door, come to another. Red turns to look at me. Her palm is clammy, cold, but her breath on my face is hot, electric. She does not speak but motions me to be quiet. Her finger to her lips hushes me like one sad, hallowed note. I feel guilty for no reason, the way I would when

I was forced to go to church with relatives when I was a kid. She pulls an old iron skeleton key from her dress, puts it in the slot in the door, and turns it. Before we enter she takes the bottle of whiskey from my good hand, sets it on the hallway floor. My bad hand she keeps jailed in her long fingers. We walk into the room, and it's Maggie.

She is lying in a large old American Craftsman-style bed, an elegant vessel contrary to the hard rusticity of the rest of the house. She looks dead, but powerful. There is a luminescent presence about her that makes her stronger than any person I have ever seen. There are quilts pulled up to her neck. Her hair and face are white. Her eyes are closed. The lines in her cheeks and neck are deep valleys of time. There is a trace of red in her lips. I see no rising and falling of her chest beneath the covers. She looks as though she has been lying here just like this for years. Waiting. Somehow I know it is her, even though I have never seen a picture, and it dawns on me then that it is odd that Hal would not have kept one single photograph of her, at least that I knew of or could find after he died. We are at the foot of the bed. I move closer. Red stops me. I have never in my life seen such saturnine heaviness in a face. Her eyes are hungry tigers. Better men would try to kiss her. I try to wriggle my hand away, but she won't let go.

She takes me out of the room. Locks the door. Key to her dress. I begin to say something, to protest, but she plugs my mouth with the fingers of her free hand, and without much effort, I am her prisoner. She leads me back to the staircase, but before we move I reach down for the whiskey. She looks at me and shakes her head no. I take the bottle anyway.

In the kitchen. Bottle on the dusty table. All fingers in her fingers. She washes my hands in the sink, scrubbing them. The water comes out rusty for a few seconds, as red as Red's hair before going clear. I do not smell God in the air.

After she dries my hands I go for the bottle. She stops me.

"Whiskey," I say, and my throat burns as if I had just plugged the grain.

She stares at me blankly before her eyes go to fog.

"Talk," I say.

She shakes her head no.

"I won't go for the bottle if you start talking."

Her head side-to-side in the negative. I reach for the bottle and she screams. I leave it be. I reach for it again. She screams. I run my hand back and forth for the bottle, conducting a symphony with her cries, each time I get close to it, she screams.

"Forget it," I say.

She smiles.

I think of Maggie up there tucked tenderly into the mouth of death. "Is she. You know. Is she gone?"

Red, the lone prairie's own sensuous enigma, just shrugs. Then she leaves the house.

After the door closes behind her I snatch up the bourbon and full of pride and shame screw it into my mouth with sad ecstasy. Nearly puking, I set it back down and go after her, pausing only for a quick look in the living room. The piano. As I approach it I notice the grandfather clock. It is staring at me with eyes slit like crucial veins. I know the face of the clock. I know it too well. I move closer to it, and its face is Hal's face.

I see Red out snooping around the Hondo. She goes for the trunk but it doesn't give. She gets in the car. She's in the backseat. She's in the front seat. She takes up Hal's finger bones and studies them, not understanding a thing about them for all I can tell. She blows into them like into dice, sets them back on the dash. Maybe she understands. She gets in the backseat again. Then she gets out. Then she vanishes. Just like that. My eyes burn, my throat is a closed sphincter. She reappears over at the fallen barn. Just like that. She looks ten years younger. Her dress is torn. I walk over to her, no longer trusting anything of this world. I go back into the house, get the bottle, and join her.

"Scream all you want," I say. And I drink.

She is silent, and there is bright warmth coming out of her, radiating directly from her skin, a light cutting through the sorry gray and rubbing my cheeks hot.

"So here we are. Abel's last stand." *Whoever kills Hal will suffer a sevenfold vengeance.* I swallow hard from the bottle and then pour one on the rubble. "For Cyrus," I say. I say, "The brother. The son. The holy ghost."

She picks up a sliver of wood from the rubble and with it carves into the black dirt. I read it: "The father."

"Not God," I say. "I've met him."

Red takes the bottle from my hand and right when I think she's going to dump it, she guzzles it. The girl just takes it down, a pro. A better man would have kissed her there, right at the foot of the memorial. I look up into the walnut trees. Crows, laughing. A lot of them. I bring my eyes down and again she is gone, the empty fifth spinning in the dirt, wiping out her scribed words, and the wind growing, growling.

She is back in the house, looking at me through the eyes of the second story. I go back in and meet her upstairs. She takes me by the hands into the other room. There is a child's bed and a reclining chair in the corner positioned to keep vigil on the bed. Nothing else. The room was started but never finished. She sits me down on the old chair, all matted and greasy with coiled springs winding up through the ass, so brittle I think it's going to collapse below me, but it holds. She shifts me back into it and leaves the room. A few minutes later she returns and in her hands is Hal's cedar box. She puts the box on the bed and opens it. She comes to me and runs her fingers through the natty wilds of my beard. She smiles down on me the smile of a proud mother who has just found her child rolling in mud, as if I were a miracle worth the burden. Next, she goes to the bed and with an ancient user's deft hand she cooks the heroin, ties me off, finds the vein, and puts the plunger to the rush.

124

The dust on the walls, the dust covering everything, dissolves into holy blue. The hairs on my arms, the back of my neck, dance. A sea of little brown devils. My lungs are cold, my armpits full of fever. I look at the emptiness of my old finger. There is ache in my heart but admittedly just a faint little less. The hazel gauze envelops. The emptiness seems far away, one lone game bird narrowly escaping into the distance. It is the only time I have ever had heroin, the only time it has ever had me. I never could understand Hal's fixation with it—the closest he could ever come to explaining it was that for him it was like what he assumed The Blues to be: a comforting, strident way to belt the hard scrabble of life—and sitting there high and watching time melt right in front of my slit eyes I begin to get a better idea of it.

*Do— you— know— why— I— am— here?* The words slide out of my mouth slow and wet as birthed sloth.

*Do you know why I am here?* she asks.

*You can talk. I'll be goddamned.*

*No. I can't. I am not talking.*

*But I can hear you,* I say. Her voice is honeyed, velvet, an Irish lament. *I can see your lips move.*

*I don't have any lips.*

*Okay.*

*Then you're not there, either. I understand.*

*Here.*

*Where?*

*Here. We are not there. There is no there. Only here.*

*Yes, here,* I say.

*How do you feel?*

*Medieval. Like chamber music.* I sink into it, soft but dark strings and winds through the lift. *Like cool sin. Like warm milk and razor blades.*

*The middle word in 'medieval' is 'die,'* she says. *Do you like the music?*

I do not answer her.

*There is a piano downstairs.*

*I know*, I say.

*No. You do not know*, she says.

I remember again why I am here. *That is Maggie, right? In the other room?*

*Yes.*

*Is she dead?*

*Not yet*, she says. Then, time reenters the atmosphere with a meteoric burn. She says, TOMORROWSHEDIES BUT NO NOTALONE, silver and quick, and just before I move in to kiss her I pass out.

When I come to I am in the bathroom, sitting back against the toilet, a hot towel around my neck, and a face full of lather. My eyes open, wounded to the light. I feel the urgent need to puke but I cannot move. I have never felt so sick, so toothless, so rotten with nausea. The woman is shaving me. She has gone through almost three years of beard with shears, readies herself with the blade. She uses a straight razor, and I think of Hal's right finger. Not a fret finger, not at all like mine. His rig finger, but still. Not his Maggie finger.

"A right finger is not a left finger," I say.

"Don't move," she says.

"A rig finger is not a fret finger."

"Quiet."

"I am a guitar player," I say. "I was. A guitar player. I was."

"Quit talking. I need to finish. Time is short."

I feel weak, sucked dry. I raise the nub, wiggle it. "I used to play the hell out of the guitar. It was what I was good at. I lost this finger, my fret hand. I lost the wrong finger on the wrong hand."

"Why are you telling me things we both already know?"

"Hal lost the wrong finger, too."

"Who's Hal?"

126

"You mean, you don't know?"

"No," she says.

"But that is Maggie up there."

"Yes, yes. Maggie. Yes."

"Who are you?"

"Me?" she says, as if contemplating it more for herself. I wait for the answer, trying my damnedest to shirk the overwhelming pulse to lose my stomach. The bathroom is silenced as if in a vacuum, devoid of gravity, suspended someplace between belief and disbelief. I am stoned and scared, feeling unreal with levitation but all too real with the queasiness sucking up out of the abyss. She breathes deep. With suspension she holds her breath and we are underwater. Her neck tightens and the tendons stick far out until she exhales and they fall back in line with the rest of her gorgeous column of flesh. We surface. "I," she says. "I am the unborn."

She goes in with the razor and I nod out.

I woke up in the Hondo. It was still parked at the edge of the weedy driveway. I picked up Hal's knuckle bones, rattled them in my hand. I pulled up my sleeve: one red dot circled in bruise, needlepoint, a microscopic nip of a more calculating she-wolf. I found the box in the backseat, everything there, the hypodermic, the Zippo, spoon, cotton balls, everything except for the dope. I looked in the mirror: not one hair on my face. I looked young, handsome even, though in my eyes there still resided the rapt terror of such sad madness. But only in the eyes.

I got out of the car and surveyed the farm. Night was coming. The wind had stopped and the air was again hot with summer. This one day felt like thirty-three. I could smell God stronger than ever, scorching the ruin with his desert stink. I called for the girl but there was no sign of her. She was gone. The air tasted of the tangy metallic emptiness of departure. There was no sign of anything in the house, not even our footprints in the dust. All of the cobwebs were intact. I went into the bathroom and there was nothing but porcelain and copper vacancy, no towel, not a single hair in the sink or on the floor, each coated in undisturbed dust. It was as if I had never set foot in the house, even though I knew the rooms. I thought of Maggie upstairs alone and dressed for the pyre, waiting on the train that blew the station lifetimes ago. I turned the water on in the sink and it coughed and bled violent clots of rust before going fluid and clear. I tried the sink in the kitchen which did the same. I went back into the bathroom and looked in the mirror. I had face.

I thought, *The unborn.*

I had face.

I was clean shaven and ready to face God.

# Chapter Four

I went upstairs to see about Maggie. The skeleton key was sitting on the banister in the hallway. Coated in dust, but I didn't need it anyway. The door was open. She looked the same, an elegant vessel put to the test, one hand on the stock, knocking on heaven's door. I watched her for a while from the doorway, rubbing my fingers through the space in front of my neck where my beard once grew. I moved to get closer and she turned her head. A slick of yellow bile dribbled from the corner of her mouth and onto the pillow, and it sent me sailing back down the stairs, out the door, and into the Hondo. The flight of the intruder: Now I was coyote. Thief coming for the take, though I hadn't yet realized what exactly it was that I was stealing. Again my body went to nerves. I was courting too much death: Hal, Maggie, the world. My own? And the girl, what of her? Was she real? What's "real?" There's no middle word in "real."

I got out of the car, moved to the trunk, and fished for the whiskey. There was the gun, the cock come home to roost. Who the hell was I to come all the way here and alter this woman's final days with a silver bullet from the past? I had not even thought of Maggie. Only Hal, only myself. I got back in the car and took down a third of a bottle, wrestling with the front seat, the steering wheel, the key in the ignition. I stared out the window. The farm was so busted. I got out and called for the girl again, but it was just nothing. Somehow I knew she wouldn't be back even though I wasn't sure of anything anymore. I rubbed the smooth skin of my neck, my cheekbones. Delivering the letter could be seen as altering fate, but truth outlives truth. Screw fate, I decided, once and for all. It does not exist. I had come this far. Maybe God does exist—*that*, by our convictions, we might allow, or *it* might allow us—but not fate. One more swig, and I went back into the house. Bottle in hand.

I turned the lights on. Electricity still pumped through the farm's veins. Someone was paying the bills. Darkness was descending, and it was still hot. I moved to open some windows but they were nailed shut. Retracing the house, I could now make out a few paths of footsteps in the dust, besides mine from earlier though not mine or the bare feet of the girl from before, of which there was no evidence whatsoever, but others. Small loafers coated in a lighter dust than the rest of the house. I bent down to study them when I heard her call from the bed.

"Gloria? Gloria?" Maggie's voice was strained, a death throb, sick and beautiful. Deep, smoky, authoritative and weighted, a survivor's chord tinged with the silica of God.

"Ma'am."

"Who is that? Who is that right now?"

"It's not Gloria," I said, and I walked up the stairs.

When I got to the foot of the bed she raised her head and studied me with glossed velvet green eyes. She looked long and hard enough. She said: "You're no angel."

"Not really," I said. "No."

"Then be gone with you. I've no business. I'm not living, I'm dying. I'm not buying, and I am not in any fashion selling."

I could tell that it hurt her to talk, that it took whatever dwindling juice that lay in her old battery to make a slow, revving point.

"Me neither," I said.

"Who sent you? Where's Gloria?" She coughed between the words.

I wanted to tell her that Hal had sent me. Or that it was God's business. But the reality, it turns out (I realized after an initial inability to answer without thinking really hard about it) is that I had come on my own. "Nobody," I said. "I came on my own accord."

"Well, what do you want? I'm busy." She was tough. Ninety-percent gone but full of salt. Yet the embers were cooling. The coughing churned with violence, her organs up in her throat and her tongue swollen and caught in the trap of her teeth. She hacked a clot of blood the size of a large date. It tumbled out of her mouth and landed on the quilt. Her lips and her chin were speckled with red. Her eyes were wet with the strain. I stared at the clot. It sat there like a miscarried fetus, brown and sad. When I looked back at Maggie she was out, the air going in and out of her in measured clicks with long intervals in between.

I stood by the bed and drank whiskey until she came back around about an hour or so later.

"Well?" she said.

"Who's Gloria?" I asked.

"She comes," Maggie hacked, "every other day or so to check on me. To feed and water me." On a table next to the bed was an old ceramic basin full of water with a rubber tube extending between it and the pillow. Next to it, a plate of crackers and some type of geriatric vitamin paste. Beneath the table were bottles of water. On the floor between the table and the bed was a silver bedpan.

"A nurse?"

"A friend. She is a good friend. The only friend. Only one

left, anyway." Maggie sucked on the tube, took some water, then coughed most of it back out.

"I had a friend once, too," I said.

"Who are you?"

She coughed up another clot, smaller than the first but bright with syrupy red. Shaking with the effort, she slid her body to the side and more of the yellow bile came, this time some of it dripped from her nose. She pulled on the quilt. The first clot, now dried, fell to the floor. I casually slid my foot over and with the tip of my shoe slid it under the bed.

She took a few minutes to get her bearings, sipping from the tube as best she could. I was afraid to help her. I was afraid to touch her. I had come this far and I was just petrified. She said, "You're still here?"

"I'm sorry to bother you. I came because this friend of mine. H...he. He lived his life by the memory of a woman he loved all the way until his life ran out on him, and I'm here. To. Pay my respects, I suppose, and. To deliver this." I took the letter out of my pocket and set it on the table next to the bed.

"You afraid of an old woman, boy? You're shaking in the skillet. I'm half dead. More than half. You're still in the fryer. Get on with it."

"This man, you know. He lived by your memory. He loved you, for all time."

"I do not know what in God's name you are talking about."

"H—"

"This some secret fancy? Ol' Doyle Steward down on Jephtha Lake? Well, whoever it is, it's long past too late. Look at me."

"Someone else." I was talking about Hal, but I thought of Red: naked, coming up out of the waters of Jephtha, wherever that was and whichever vow it was bound to. I ached for her as if she were the sole instrument. I was trembling again. It was difficult to talk. My throat was constricting, swallowing on

132

itself. I took a drink of whiskey, stammered, clearing the rising burn. "This friend. He. You know. No matter what. Happened. I guess you should know he loved you until the end."

Her pupils pinned and her face turned when I said "the end." She was already white as chalk, and now her ghost flashed to the fore, and she yellowed. She was quiet for some time. Then she said, "Give me that." I moved to hand her the letter. "Not that, sir. The bottle. Pass it over."

I set the whiskey down on the floor behind the chair. "I don't know."

"Give it to me. Please."

It had been my medicine, I had so convinced myself. "Medicine," I said, more to myself.

"Yes, medicine," she said and started coughing brutally. With one great jerking wheeze she inhaled deep and exhaled a river of blood, down her gown and all over the quilt. A pint of it. She did not breathe afterward for what seemed like five minutes. She was in another place all her own as I wiped up the blood with a rag I found sitting next to the water basin.

"Are you all right?" I thought she had died.

"Yes. Just give me the bottle."

"Are you sure?"

"Am I speaking clear? How is my intonation? I said give me the damn bottle." The words came slow but clear. She was breathing hard, trying to keep the air in the room going in and out of her lungs long enough to finish her sentences. "I'll be dead by dawn. I should be. Either that or I'll live another hundred years. Make it easier on me, will you." Then she said, and it was very eerie, she said, "You may be an angel yet."

"Intonation..." I said. I thought of the guitar. The harmonics, the mechanics of a guitar. Then I thought of the mechanics of death and wondered if someone really can see it come galloping down off of the sphere.

"What about it?"

"I can hear you," I said.

"You sure?"

"No."

"Of all the nerve, coming here. Give me the bottle."

"I don't know."

"Don't be such a damn cur," she said, and I realized even more right then how deep love runs sometimes, despite silence, science, or even religion. Intersecting lines beyond such futile ideas of time, fate, and destiny, but total emotion. I mean, thee clay, the earth.

"I should go," I said.

"Leave it on the table."

"I already did."

"Forget the letter. The bottle, boy. What's in it?"

"Ah," I said, picking it up and raising it to the crescent of light from the old fixture above the bed. "Whiskey it be."

"My eyes aren't so good these days. Pass it over," she said. "And sit down."

I handed her the bottle but she was too weak to hold it. So I unscrewed it and raised it to her, a shot's worth, some of it going in, some of it dribbling out the sides of her mouth and mixing with the crusting yellow trail of bile. I may have been an alcoholic, but I knew enough to stop when there was yellow bile. Blood is one thing. Blood and whiskey are brothers. Sometimes good, sometimes bad, but forever intertwined. But yellow bile, no ma'am. In her condition, this was suicide. Yet I gave it to her anyway. She had an authority about her that I could not defy.

"Just leave it by the pillow," she said. "And sit."

I obeyed. I pulled a chair that was sitting in the corner up to the bedside. Then, full of shame, with my shirtsleeves I began to clean the rest of the vital humors from her face, neck, gown, and quilt. I poured some of the water from the basin onto the shirt and rubbed it out, then wrung it into the bedpan.

"Thank you."

"It's okay," I said.

"I apologize. I do not mean to be rash. I'm short on patience. I've been dying for a long time. People come around, wanting to buy, as if a price could be put on something," she said, "as lived-in as this old farm."

"It's okay," I said. Now I know: There is no "okay," God.

"Do you expect me to believe myself when I imagine who it is you are talking about? I have, mind you, been suffering dementia in these last days."

"Me, too," I said.

"So he's gone," she said. "Finally."

"Yes. A few days ago. I buried him in California."

"California?"

"Yes. He was my neighbor. In Los Angeles," I said. Then I said, "He was my friend."

"Los Angeles. Well."

"I guess you didn't know? I mean even where he lived?"

"I haven't heard a word for, lo, about forty years. For all I knew he could have been dead just as long. Though somehow I knew he was not."

"He always, I believe, I truly do, he always wanted to be back here. I think he stayed in Los Angeles to punish himself," I said. I looked at my fingers. Neither of us had yet spoken his name.

"Hal," Maggie said.

"Yes," I said, "Hal."

"He punished more than himself," she said.

"Yes. I guess he did."

It took her about a full minute to put her hand to the bottle, but she got it, and, fighting the shakes with every breath, spilling some of it on the pillow, she took a drink on her own. "It burns," she said and again started a fit of coughing. When she finally caught her breath she said, "But it burns anyway, so why not. It's a good burn. For once."

"It is a good burn."

She looked out the window. "I wish we were there."

"Los Angeles?"

"Yes. Never been. Never even been to California period. Maybe that's why he chose it, knowing I'd never make it far enough away from home. I don't know. Guess I'll never really know. Might as well have gone to China, no difference. I'd just like to see it, I guess, see what he surrendered to."

"It's my home," I said. "I think. But, then again, you can never truly own Los Angeles, or California. She owns you. The bear eats you." Even so, I missed it already, as if I would never return. Strange how you can so deeply miss something that took so much from you.

"What did he tell you?"

"Everything, I think."

"I was always faithful," she said.

"No two people have the same idea of a story," I said.

"It's true. About Cyrus—his brother. We did have private relations. Just that once. But it's not what you think."

"I'm not here to judge. I'm just here doing something for a friend." It was in that moment, somewhere wedged into the latter part of that second sentence, that, with rawboned insight, I did wonder why I was there, and I knew it was for far more selfish reasons than just to do something kind for a friend. "And to do something for myself. I've wasted a lot of time in Los Angeles."

"You're young, young man. You have time."

"Do you believe in God?"

"Oh, I suppose," she laughed. I could see the blood come up to her lips and watched her swallow it back down. "Why not."

"What if I told you I heard God laugh. That he laughed at me? Twice. Just a few days ago. And again yesterday. On my

136

way here. Just opened up his mouth like a nuclear warhead and rattled my bones, the aftershock chasing me all the way here from Arizona. I could see them, the rings of aftershock waving through the desert hotter than heat, and then again in Nebraska, just like in an old film of atom bombs. That ripple after impact. That roll of wave before the onslaught, stopping time for a second so you can watch it coming for you, the crest of the unknown, frightening and almost pretty. No mushroom clouds, though. Only ringing silence ensuing like I've never known. Like the death of music."

She thought about it for a few minutes. "Well," she said, "having lived my life, I might just laugh right back. Either that or start prayin', and hard."

"I'm a guitar player. I was. I can't play no more on account of this. I lost it, bit off by a dog. I almost killed myself without even trying. And. Hal. Hal, he took me in."

I showed her the nub. I held it up, wiggled it, kept the other fingers on the hand flush, then fisted. She did not say anything about it for a while until she said, "There's a piano downstairs."

Then she choked out another sheet of blood and fell asleep.

I did not stop to visit my parents on the way through Chicago. I do not know why. Iowa had been nothing but a painted beige blur. When I crossed the Illinois line I drank. I drove fast with the windows down screaming my head off, no longer caring at all about the police, half-wishing I would get caught just so I might be brought back into a different reality. But there wasn't one. As I skirted down below the tip of Lake Michigan, past the birth land and the first death land and into the stinking infernos of Gary, Indiana, I waited gingerly for the hyoid of God to produce, separating the men from the apes. The loved from the unloved. The feared from the fearful. The on-key from the flat. The sound full from the silent. There was nothing but the wind bitching with heat through all of the open windows, toasting my whiskey and tangling my beard with sweat, and the cursed silence of a stolen radio, not even the slightest bridge for fealty. He was playing on his own terms. I could laugh until my larynx popped and it wouldn't matter. I could yowl out blasphemies all over the flatlands of my history. I could even curse God. I could say things like, "Epiphany is evolution spelled backwards!" or "God is a eunuch," or "Here's what I've decided: You may have invented life, but you can't control it. That's why you have to destroy it over and over and over again. Fine. But we are creatures of conscience, your most imperfect creation. No divinely innocent creature of the earth might suffer—those without conscience—unless for your mistakes. Canine slave lust! Totally natural! And I don't need any crap about the animal kingdom solely at harvest as the dominion of man. Nope. Not entirely, anyway. The jig is up. The German shepherd had no moral doubt. Do this, do that. Bite finger. Do dogs objurgate? But the kicker is, when humans are incapable of understanding it all due to more of your failures as a geneticist, what do we call them? Angels. We say they are angels. Fuck... They. They die truly alone."

I could scream all of this stuff up into the dusk with no rebuke, which I did. Or something like it anyway, driving fast and drunk, trying to hold her steady. Remember, I called to the clouds, that the future is the past, the dirt is God, there is no science there is only music, good night and what comes tomorrow.

I awoke at the piano a few hours before dawn. I'd let Maggie rest for the night. I'd gone out to the car for the last fifth. It didn't take much to get on since two-thirds emptiness of the bottle I left with her was hot wire spliced through my veins. Out there, I stood wolf-eyed and swallowed the midnight stars. The sky was clear, the air hot, distended onward with humidity. There were crickets everywhere, a hundred-thousand fucking violins humping with fever in the moonlight. It was euphonic and menacing all at once. Calculated and chaotic, a hypnotic frenzy. I bathed in it like an electric eel until it fulminated in the casus belli: A sluice of rain and hail came with the thunder of spooked horses, belting me until I was soaked to the guts and bruised cold before the gauntlet: no ozone, no petrichor, nothing but the smell of dry rotting desert seething at high noon, fossilizing to a putrid crisp. In the Midwest a ninety-degree melt can rail into frigid balls of ice without warning and not even stinking of the bitter cold, I now know because of God infesting my nostrils. The hail grew to the size of ripened grapefruits before it cleared, and I saw him there strung up in the walnut trees with a halo of pink moon lit behind him: God in tatters. The same lined face but destroyed. The same clothes as in Nebraska, shredded. He had been beaten and burned, hung like a ghoulish melted crucifix bought at a fire sale. Skin blazoned with scenes of all-too-human inhuman violence. Lynched. The crows were plucking at his eyeballs, and his entrails spilled out and down to the ground where they coiled into a greasy viper of shit.

"What if they are the only ones who know with certainty the intimacies of pain, the necessity and reward of pain, and that's why they do not speak of it?"

It was difficult to watch him talk as his lips were being peeled back by the murder. "What?"

"Your question was, well, stupid. It has been asked so many exhausting times before. You should have stopped to visit your folks instead. That's why you fail. You've no focus."

"I've already buried them once. I'm not in the business of burying things twice."

"So you say."

"I'm trying to focus. I'm getting there."

"I'm sure," God said.

"Quit following me," I said.

"Why do you treat me as if I am your hunter?"

One of the crows tugged at bits of God's exposed liver and tossed them in the air once before wolfing them down. "Are you going to make it?"

"I do not feel a thing. Would you like to know why?"

"Pray-tell," I said.

"Because I know the true nature of death. Those beasts, those angels, they do not die alone."

"Pray-tell," I said.

And God laughed a simple hoot, gamely, as if between two best friends hotly pursuing the same girl. hAMen. The crows with unknown silence wrapped him back up, sewed him all back together again, cleaned the wounds, a flurry of smutty nurses with slick wings stitching until he just sat up there in the tree looking the same as he did when I first saw him in the dream. Relaxed as a wise old junkie high and with zero regret.

"I challenge you to a duel," he said.

Then he was gone, no trace of rain or hail on the ground and the crows, the crows, the crows, the lot of them: looking lustfully at me with dry black eyes cutting through damp black night, hoping I would be carrion before long, heads twitching in anticipation of a reward.

I went back to the car and retrieved the gun. One slug left. I almost let them have it, fucking crows. They were laughing at me, smiles on their beaks long and starched as dried corn cobs. I sucked on the whiskey and laughed back, but it did not come out right. I was a bad actor acting as if I was in on their game, a blind audition, ha ha har ha. Still, I held fast. I wasn't going to waste it on God this time, either. Or at least not yet.

I was soaking wet, but when I crossed into the house I was dry to the bone. *His work*. I walked over to the piano, wiped the dust off with my shirtsleeves. Hal smiled down on me from the grandfather clock. I had a drink. Then I opened the case of the clock and poured one for Hal into his dust and chains. I found the key and wound him, set the ticker to rock. I laid the gun across the upright back of the piano, tugged on the whiskey, and put my fingers to the keys. I was feeling sad and dangerous. The hammers hit the strings with unthinkable warmth. I stretched my fingers, the knuckles cracking. The nub wriggling forward to meet the ivory along with the others, trying almost independent of my hand. I ran a rusty scale, found some awkward chords, and felt the good shiver of happiness prick up my spine. I thrummed along the keys, getting to know them. I cleared my throat, put it to a note, and then I just let it roll, starting with my own "Brighter Dark, Baby:"

> I was born six hundred years ago
> In the gut of Chicago
>
> I known since day one, baby, you
> Sucked crime from the marrow
>
> The cold wolves in the yard
> Startin' to howl
>
> You and I, baby, come tomorrow
> In the brighter dark, we'll screw everyone

It was the first time I had sung anything since my last show. I could not even remember the last time I had even hummed a bona fide tune, I had been so exiled from purpose and estranged from any vehicle of song for so long.

Reckless and foaming for the fix, abandoned to the creation of sound, I played more, screwing most of them up, far from able to do to the piano what I once did with the guitar but knowing myself what they were. With each tune I took a belt from the bottle: "Tomorrow will Come," "My Once Desire," "You're Gonna Wonder about Me," "Next Rider," "Princes and Whores," "I Crawled," "To Bleed Together," "You're Gonna Be

Sorry You Let Me Down," "You're Gonna Wish Twice More," "Black Angels," "I Deserve to be Mean," "Those Who Know," "It Ain't My Luck I'm Worried About," "Times Change, but I Don't," and "Esoteric" (*But the sun / is a sucker / and the water sucks up the sun / but the moon gives out the water / and cats eat birds / so they can fly*)—straightforward but lasting songs I had at one time played forever, standards now askew with my cuckooed fury and the rust of hands silenced by such a fruitless slag of time. It was all the old raw milk and razor wire, utterly wonderful. I was enraptured with the jawed sound. The piano had gone out of tune long ago, and I didn't give a good god-damn. Hal unfrozen and timeless kept time, chiming the beat, the pendulum pulsing within his tower like an old heart kicking still. I played until I passed out.

There was still almost half a fifth of whiskey left when I woke up. My lungs were scorched, my vocal chords shredded. Hal at rest, the ticker had ceased. At least for now. The light was coming up. I went up to Maggie's room to see if she was still alive.

# Chapter Five

"**M**Y husband played the piano."

"You remarried?"

"What was I supposed to do," she coughed. "Don't get self-righteous with me."

"I'm not. I'm just interested."

"I haven't talked this much in years it seems." Maggie constantly cleared the phlegm and blood and bile and whatever other juices of infirmity that were rising up. "It's too much work. I don't like to talk. Not anymore."

"You made it past dawn," I said.

"It'll be my last," she said. "Did you bury him?"

"Not in Los Angeles. I took him north, along the ocean, to a place called San Simeon. There was a lighthouse there that he liked. I took him there. I took him there and I burned him."

A flash of blue lit on her face, the cold blue of vulgar fear.

"Then I put his ashes into the Pacific Ocean."

Her brow dropped and it dawned on me that I had never even considered bringing his remains home. I perhaps, genuinely, never felt worse in my conscience than I did with this thought.

"He used to work the lighthouse here, in South Haven."

"I know," I said.

Maggie took a drink of water from her tube, swallowed, then slid the tube out of the basin. She was trying to bring it across her chest, all the way onto the bed, but it was not easy. I moved to help her but her eyes arrested me. It took her about twenty minutes to do it, which is an insanely long time when you're just sitting there watching someone take painstaking effort while feeling helpless yourself, in addition to the waxing fact that the world was for all I knew going to end tomorrow. Maybe even tonight at midnight. God hadn't specified the hour, only the day. Maggie got the tube all the way across and into the whiskey bottle I'd left there the night before. She swallowed hard, choked, chased down another breath enough to go again, and took it down. It was about six in the morning.

"I guess you know him even better than I do," she said.

"No. I know him because of you, *through* you, and that's about all I know of him," I said. "After you, after Cyrus, he became a demon on the long road to hell. That's who I knew, the forever cursed. Some poor pawn at the mercy of Mount Olympus."

"He was a good man," she said. "He loved so much."

"He never stopped. With you."

"He should have stayed. I did not like Cyrus. You have to understand. I loved him dearly, he was family, but I never liked him too much. I never, ever, wished him dead, mind you, but he was all flash. Except for that claw. Too slick for his own britches, so he thought. But Hal, Hal was the best of man, kind and true but hardened, too. Even if he could not have helped pulling that trigger, he should have stayed. Should have come back."

"Sometimes it's just not easy to go back to what you've lost. To what you've convinced yourself you cannot ever regain," I said.

"He should have, anyway. How does one ever know unless they try?"

"There was barely a day that went by that he didn't chastise me for it."

"For what?"

"For not trying. To play the guitar again. I don't expect you to understand, because nobody seems to. Except. Except, Hal. He understood because he couldn't return to the source of his own loss. He couldn't return to this place. He couldn't return to you. Yet, he had to have known it was a possibility. Maybe a long shot. Because he didn't simply shrug off my loss with blind enthusiasm, you know, 'Buck up, you can do it!' That kind of stuff. Don't get me wrong, he sure made me feel stupid for sitting there wallowing in my defeat while so much actual death cascades all around us like so much weather. He'd rub my face in it and pretend his own was clean."

"Death, sir. It does descend. But it also rises up," and with that Maggie blew a terror of fluid all over the opposite side of the bed and onto the wall. She went out like hot piss on good fire. I sat and stared at the drying stains, bits of sputum. She was out for about two hours, but when she came to she said, "And so."

"I thought that was it."

"I do not remember what we last said."

"No, you," I said. "I thought. That."

"Death decides the loose time frame. But I'm going to make the final call," she said. "What about this guitar?"

"Okay. Well, see. This finger. It's the one you put on the frets, on the neck of the guitar, if you're right-handed like me. You run it up and down the neck like this. It's the most important one, and when I lost it, it scrambled up everything for me. And a lot of nice people, they wanted to coach me. They were just trying to help, but I did not want to hear it. Even though

145

it's true, they had their points: I could learn to play left-handed. I could get a prosthetic nub to make do, might even create a new sound, a new run with it. But I just couldn't. I was never in it for the money or any kind of fame. Playing made me feel I could actually transmit something valid within this world, both out of and back into myself, and losing the finger made me an excommunicated mess. And Hal, no matter how much he hauled me over the coals about it, understood. He understood because he understood love. He understood what it is to love something with everything you are. He understood that the loss of love is the loss of love, no matter what that love is for, and, on top of literally saving my life, my living flesh, he broke it that way to try to save my soul. And I don't mean that strictly in the old hellfire way. I mean, my spirit, my drive, my juju, my mojo, if there was any left. He tried to make an example out of himself in order to save me the trouble of going out with total loss and regret." I finally understood it.

"So, even if you're right-handed it's the left that matters? You rely on the left," she said.

"Yes. The spiral."

"I'll go out with total loss," Maggie moaned. "But no regret."

We both dozed off for a minute after we fell silent for a time.

"Hal had a missing toe—"

"Lawnmower accident," she said. "Just before we were married."

"Oh." It was a letdown. Hal had never told me where the toe went, and I had hoped it was by some grand adventure on the high seas of despair and glory. I decided not to tell her about his finger.

She tugged another slug from her whiskey tube, and I reached down for my own fifth and took a sip.

"Hal wanted more than anything in the world to have a

baby. But something wasn't going right. We tried. For years, we did. Family was something then, especially around here. It was the biggest thing. But our number just wouldn't come up. We went and talked to doctors over in Allegan and even a specialist in Kalamazoo. Well, the results came back. I got them in the mail while Hal was out working the boats. It wasn't me, it was him. Hal's. His. See," she choked, "his sperm was all wrong. He could not get me pregnant. But he wanted that baby so bad. A whole crop of children, that was our talk. The tall dream."

A drain of tears ran down her face and met with the paste at her lips. Her skin was sunken in the jaws, bloated at the cheeks, with eyes gone more black than brown from their autumn green, her nose dry and her lips cracked, there was the blood and bits of guts on the wall ("Don't bother," she had said when I finally moved to clean it up, "we don't have time."), and still she was one of the most stunning women I have ever seen. As she tried to control her consciousness, struggling against the war in her throat, in her lungs and heart, and wanting no help from me, I imagined her younger. Hal's bride, even his widow because strangely, unfairly but honestly, sometimes women look the most beautiful when they are at their most sad, and just as I tried to conjure the image I saw it across the room: a framed photo of her standing in a blue dress in a green field in a Michigan that existed too long ago. And she was beyond stunning, a dream, the wild deer-at-the-ready eyes and dancing auburn hair of an Olde Irish goddess, her nose a perfect tilt, and lithe ruby lips parted slightly as if unexpectedly caught in the heat of a good mischievous run. It was a picture you could fall in love with, build a whole fantasy around.

"While we were engaged," she said. "When that picture was taken."

"Hum," I said, and my cheeks smarted red.

"I couldn't tell him. Oh, we talked hypothetically about adoption if it didn't work out, all of that, but you could tell the dream was on the verge of collapse. Like some great civilization running out of resources. Run out of luck. So. I. I turned to Cyrus. Only to give Hal what we both so desperately wanted. Cyrus was a shyster, and we tangled like badgers, but he loved Hal deeply so, and me, too, when all was said and done. Family was, after all, family. So. I laid down with Cyrus in the barn. I wouldn't do it with him in the house. The barn was the workplace, and this was work. A job to be done. This was before all the tricks they have today to get a woman pregnant without sullying herself. And without her husband's consent. Or at least that I could privately afford and could get away with without Hal knowing the awful truth about his impotent soldiers. Cyrus and Hal looked enough alike, were enough alike in so many ways—though Hal the better man without any of the fool monkey business Cyrus was prone to—that there would be no suspicion. I did it for Hal," she bawled, and now I was her minister. "I was ever faithful. Not so simple in the end."

Though she shook her head no, I reached toward the shock of her failing face and wiped the tears with my shirtsleeves. My own desiccated eyeballs grew wet. We each went for our respective whiskey.

"But there was never any chance to explain. In the barn. It happened so fast, everything. Everything changed just like that, forever. I was too shocked to explain myself."

I thought God the most savage puppeteer. Then I thought him helpless and sad right along with us, in our own image, we of Him. Who had cheated on God? Before us? Before Lucifer? Who could He have loved so? So that we all of us must know this unequivocal pain? The impotent God, God's well-meaning but deceitful wife.

"There wasn't really ever a farm anymore. I mean, for me. We—my father, mother, sister, and I—rented out the small house until I remarried, and we anonymously put Hal's mother into a nursing home. I did remarry some time after. Years went by. They. The years. They went by."

"Doyle Steward?" I asked.

"No. He tried, lordy did he. Soon as he heard the news. Doyle was a good man, but it was too soon. Ten years was too soon. I got married to a nice man name of Samuel Turner, long after Hal had become a ghost. I am not going to lie and say that we did not have good times, Sam and I, but things are never much the same once you experience the loss that I did on that day in that barn, the exacting death I experienced from the man whom all the while I was only trying to give life to." Something changed in her voice, the larger part of it slipped over the edge and into the abyss. The light outside had turned charcoal with black clouds, and the humidity climbed as we baked in Maggie's oven. She sucked on the tube. She did not gag anymore, just moaned the hollow thrum and sucked her own blood from the edge of her teeth and back down inside of her.

"Take it easy," I said.

"No," she said. "You take it easy. This is my time, not y'orn. Drink up."

I did. "What happened to Samuel?"

"Cancer. Ate him slow, so slow. Hal had left so fast. I didn't entirely know what time was capable of until Samuel died. The total sum of my years felt like less than the sole days of his dying. He kept the farm going until his body started turning inside out. We kept the family name on it, Conchobhar, but the farm had already lost spirit after Hal left. An honorable man, that Samuel, and he kept the Conchobhar name on it even after my folks passed and we alone took over. My sister, a single mother, moved into the old marriage house before she remarried and went to her husband's. After she left, I was here all alone. I couldn't look at that house anymore. The years added up and then divided and the quotient was worse than zero. It was misery. It was bound up in too much gravity. So, one day, all by myself, I just burnt it right on down to the ground. About ten years later the barn fell on its own bad luck. Caved in, just like a person. The silo's going, too. I couldn't run the farm anymore, nothing would grow, the help couldn't understand me and I couldn't understand them: They cared and I no longer did. So I've just been sitting here, waiting ever since."

"Waiting for Hal?"

"Heaven, no," Maggie said. "No. Just waiting."

I was sad to hear it. "He was just waiting, too."

"Not for me," she said. "It wasn't me who had gone. You know what, though? I never did divorce Hal. I married Samuel, but I never officially divorced Hal. In those days you could simply bury your problems out in the field and turn the soil, just simple country people getting on."

"Whoever ran the courts didn't catch on? I mean that you were twice married?"

"No," she said, her vocal chords tuning more to the faint. "No. The countryside was still the countryside then, in the '60s, even in the '70s, even in the '80s. Things might disappear in the city, but in the country, they just fade away and folks mind their own. At least back then."

"What was Samuel's favorite song? To play. On the piano?"

"Oh, I don't know. Ah. Well. 'That Old Time Feeling,' I guess. He liked that one. Yeah, that was the one. At least the one he played the most."

I ran it through my head. Maggie, she knew how to pick them.

"He tried his best, and it was good," she said.

"He never remarried," I said. "Hal. I don't even know if he was ever even with another woman."

"That kind of romance doesn't exist," she said, but I could tell by the look in her eyes she knew that no matter how unlikely, for some wild, rare breed of people it actually really did exist.

"How old is Gloria?" I asked.

150

"Almost my age. But going strong. Why?"

"Just wondering," I said, but I was thinking about the girl. Red.

Silence is also a tone, and there was a long tone of silence split between us. I ate some of Maggie's crackers and shifted in my seat while she lay there groaning and unevenly slurping on whiskey.

"You never got pregnant?" I finally asked. "Have any children?"

The air seemed to rush completely out of her. She dissolved further into the bed. "I did," she droned. "I did get pregnant, but I beat myself with my own fists until my stomach turned purple and I lost it. It was never born."

"God," I said.

Neither of us said anything for a while, then:

"Sir?" she said.

"Yeah?"

"The Midwest is a dark place."

"Yes," I said. "Yes it is." I thought of California, of Los Angeles, of how at least there the impotence and the violence and the miscommunication and the loss are habitually on display. And how in California the light rarely goes all the way out, even at night. The darkest hours, and there is still that little flicker buried in what you come to think is the cold.

I turned to tell Maggie about God but her eyes were closed and it seemed she had finally decided and had gone off to that other place.

"Forget it, man," Sweet Julio said. "Rock and roll, that's all it is."

"Always too much, and never enough (for you)," I said.

"Maybe for you," he said.

I'd walked in on him shooting cooked powders in the bathroom of a downtown loft some actor had converted into a showplace that we were playing, some weeks before the incident with the LAPD K-9 Unit. "No," I said. "It's The Blues." I was trying to get him to straighten out and do some recording with me. I wanted his chaos, the sound of it, but I did not need his death. He was slipping over the blurred line between the two. I took a small snort with him and hated myself for it, shucking most of it out of my nostrils.

"Exactly," he said. He licked up too much of what was going to ruin his hands for the night.

Fuck the myth. So what if every guitar player, every good one anyway, has to have a separate addiction in order to ride, the nature of the blessing and subsequent curse of playing—mine having been whiskey for a serious amount of years, and sometimes Oh yes oh those women—but things can't get too out of tune with each other or the tunes themselves flunk. Acid, blow, booze, crank, weed, wine, women. Even heroin. They've all had their stake in pushing toward unexplored greatness—chemical-courted genius—but too much of it and the music always, always suffers. Exactly the same as when things get too sober. And in death there are no fingers left. Hal knew it, he kept the harmony going right until the end, I'll give him that.

"Lonewolf," Julio said, pushing past me, "shit. You're a true wolf among wolves. A dog among dogs."

That night Sweet Julio melted right before my eyes. Then oxidized. I mean he turned to coal, a diamond reverting in on itself. Then pure rust. Dusted, just blew it, just like that, the end. The only ass he could have kicked that night was dead ass, if that, but we were playing for the living. His hands were cramped up into little lobster claws, trying to make sense of the instrument as if they had been drawn up out of the ocean and dropped into a boiling pot of Grand Ole Opry. We could all see it. He was gone, done. I got on the stage, saddened by it all, and I just shredded. I was flying on whiskey, but only just enough. I tore a blind ass through the joint, cut the room like a machete through virgin cane. An unwound raga of hot dagger Blues, I played for an hour straight without pause. I tortured all eight fingers and the two thumbs that had collectively been so good to me. I beat my guitar like a Vietnamese child. I murdered all of the music I had ever known only to resurrect it, each finger a little Christful of miracle, anarchy, and forgiveness. The sound was exactly what I had been looking for all those years.

It was the show before the last. But what I would ultimately remember most about it was not how I played. What I would remember most is Sweet Julio's eyes as I passed him on the way out. There were none.

"The Blues," he said.

"Just below hell," I said.

"Maybe," he said. "We'll see."

"Forget it," I said. "It's only rock and roll. I don't need you anymore. We'll do the next gig." When I turned to look at him his eyes were gone. He was nailed to the wall like an Aztec slave, used into uselessness, waiting for the final cut. His pincers were still jawing, looking for the chords, but his eyes had disappeared. I'm not sure if I can say it enough: they were no more. Sweet Julio was already dead. Through the empty sockets and back into his skull was nothing but the cold vacuous ether of nothingness, and it was dark.

I sat bedside for a few hours and thought of Maggie as Jesus Christ. Yea, I considered, if God was the woman I probably wouldn't be in this house maroon-eyed and smelling like rotten onions. Yea, if God was the woman it would be Bug Wallace turned into a merman on the White House lawn with gold nipples, playing and rearranging military marching tunes with forked tongues for eyeballs. Yea, if God was the woman Hal would've shot himself instead; sympathy not for the Devil, but the curious cause supreme: Love, in all its sadness and bliss, would have prevailed in one way or another. Hal would have risen again, two Jesuses and off to create a third. Yea, if God was the woman I'd sit and watch the cells multiply and divide. I'd have grown a new finger already and plucked the strings of the sun. Yea. If. Sure enough. My Vietnamese child forgiving me.

But God, sorry, was not She.

I got up to go and Maggie came back one last time from the land of the dead, howling "It's time. It's time time time time time time."

"I'll stay until it's time," I said, looking down at my bottle.

"It's time now," she said, grabbing my hand and her tired eyes begged for it: *Please kill me.*

"That's not my place."

"Oh, it is. It is," she said. "That's why you're here. You just don't know it. You came for this. You're going to help me."

"I'm through with death."

"No," Maggie said, "you're just beginning."

"It's not my business."

"Yes. You came all this way, now finish the job. Put me to rest."

"Nothing doing. I came to deliver a letter—"

"You can use the pillow," she snuffed. "It's nothing. I thought the whiskey would be enough, but it only seems to help. Now," she said.

I reached for the letter, unfolded it, and laid it next to her. "Here," I said. "I better get going."

"I'm not going to read it unless you help me after. It's time. Be the mercy. It's the right thing to do."

"This is all I have to offer," I said, pushing the letter closer to her breast. "It's what I came for, not this."

"It's all death the same," she said. "Now make it real."

"It's not my place," I said.

"You've made it your place. Be the angel, now."

"Goodbye, Maggie. I am sorry for bothering you."

I went downstairs and sat at the piano. I tried to find the chords to "That Old Time Feeling," but the last night's juice was sucked dry. I was the lobster. Hal's shotgun was still sitting atop the piano, perched like a hawk just waiting for its hood to come off so it could go to work. The clock had gone blank, faceless, with only a trace of Hal's ghost caught in the smoke of its history. The Hondo was just beyond the drive, beyond the yard, beyond the stoop, beyond the kitchen, beyond this room, beyond the threshold.

I don't know how long I sat there lost and losing it, but Maggie started screaming, rending the air with slaughter. Her throat sounded shredded by blades. Wet. I ran upstairs and she was covered in blood, her gown half off her body and the letter clutched to her face. She was writhing, gnashing herself into the bed, possessed with the lust for death, shrieking the most horrible din, interspersed with "TIME! TIME! TIME! TIME! TIME! TIME...TIME! TIME! TIME! TIME! TIME! TIME!" Through the wash of blood and bile on her breasts I could see a dark purple lake of scar from where she once was burned. Her bottle of whiskey was almost empty.

I tried to move my hands to her, but it was as if all of my fingers had been removed. I could feel not a one of them. Her screaming turned worse and I could no longer take it. I turned to leave and she hushed. She dropped the note to the floor and pulled the drinking tube around her neck, but she was too weak to shut down even the already dying breath.

"Please," she gasped, "I don't want to do it myself. Just in case."

I looked at her turning herself inside out, emptying herself of every burden of life, suffering almost alone in this dark. If God was going to go through with it tomorrow maybe he'd do best by just pouring out old Sol. Let a hit of light into the lot of us before we flamed up and out.

"Please," her words coming out as coarse smoke, "do for me

what Hal did for you."

She was right. I owed them both. I went downstairs and got the gun. Back in the room, Maggie, Saint Margaret, Our Lady, the Queen of the Damned, fell back with her eyes closed, and I put Hal's last bullet into her head.

# Chapter Six

I met God in the field at midnight.

When I turned to leave Maggie's room, to get a grip on myself before taking care of her body, I saw him out there through the window: his wooden head on the body of a deer, staring up at me from the yard with twelve points bending up out of his temples. When we made eye contact God smiled, nodded, and sprang into the field.

Both chambers were empty, but I still had the shotgun in my hand when I left the house. Some of the weeds went up to my neck and the acreage spread into a spiny labyrinth. Flashing his antlers above the brush line, God led me to a clearing about a third of a mile from the house. The place looked at peace, the second-story eyes lidded for the night, as if the whole farm was slipping into nothing more than a good night's sleep. There was no blood from where I stood. No crime. No loss. No virtue. Just a house. The rubble of the barn and even the softening silo were obscured by the sightline and the walnut trees. There was only the house.

"Twenty paces," God said. When I turned to him he had

reversed: the head of a deer on the body I'd seen in Nebraska. "Is that how you want it?"

"Why is it so ugly? That's all I want to know." My hand was hot on the trigger. I could not let the gun go. It had become my instrument.

"Why is anything?"

"I'm talking about. The end. Death. The gore of it. Even peaceful death rots to gore, and I want to know right fucking now why. Nobody should beg for death."

"Because. You people. You hunger so much." Then he was gone.

"No. No way. I'm sick of these games. This is not doing. This is not getting on. This is not."

God reappeared with only the antlers. "You make the games. Not I, and that's the fact, jackrabbit."

My head was already bogged with the weight of Maggie but it grew denser as if plied with a hefty wig. My head tilted back with heaviness, and when I reached with my bad hand I felt two slab-sided velvet ears jutting up high out of the top of my skull. My whole body began to tremor, but I still couldn't let go of the gun. I kept reaching back and forth with my left hand between the two hare ears. There was a chunk missing out of the top of the left one. With a high treble fade-in my head rang with volume. The crickets had their amps cranked. A wild dog yowled on the other side of the woods lining the field. The deer in the forest were foraging. Coyotes walked the line, licking their hot western jowls, just waiting for something to die. God's smile made a faint creak in his totem. I could hear the crows whispering in the walnut trees six-hundred yards away. Before I could figure out exactly what they were saying, the ears were gone. No sign of the wolf, other than in me.

"Could you hear it?"

I said, "The crows."

"No. The truth."

"I heard nothing, not the beat of wild animals (to lie to God is to what?), no truth, including you and your high wooden cheeks, your high junkie chops."

"You've come a long way," God said. "I have something to tell you. I'm going to let you in on a secret. You have to listen. Listen. Close: Death is death."

"That's it. Death is death?"

"You said it, brother."

"It's not that simple."

"But it is. The same goes for me, too."

"But you're so easy to blame," I said.

God said: "It's just a fucking finger."

Silence.

He said: "Yet so much more. Yet so much less."

Silence.

Then God said: "Your comment about the light, I'll consider it."

"You mean the sun?"

"Yes."

"It all has really happened," I said. "Enough."

"Yes. Yes, it has."

Here I was: a true believer. "So now what?"

"You tell me," God said.

I was voiceless, given up to the posse of the night sky, the stars staring me down like flaming arrows, nowhere left to run. Indeed it was a long walk home, and if I knew in that moment exactly where home was, I would have charged for it.

God said, "Twenty paces."

We turned back-to-back. In his heavy right hand God held the shotgun he offered me in the dream, which was in actuality the same model as Hal's. Then he showed me his enormous left hand. All the fingers were missing.

"My gun is empty," I said.

"Check your weapon, son."

I opened the break-action and checked the breech. There was one slug. It shone like a rare pearl inlay, wicked and handsome, luster polished down to its finer composite elements, badass and ready. Tuned. Tried in the sonic dock, ready to stake it all on the jury. Every harmony and trouble a single atom of gambled breath; in the purest form, nothing is more elegant than an exhale, no matter the heat, the consequence, the programmed mud of working cells, some praying for equilibrium, others screwing peace in order to survive. All life ground out of a single peppercorn of wayward matter pissing up into the coiled and sardonic grin of the microscope, battling faith for the charms of heaven. So I told myself, positive and negative, here we are. We minuend gremlins coaxing bad lunacy in the fool name of iron and heaven, sulking with fire in the unsure night like poisonous worms with nine fingers, no whiskey, and a shaved beard full of crusted salt.

"You can shoot yourself now," God said. "Otherwise, on the count of three, then twenty."

At three we marched. The heat of the night was unbearable. I had to bite at the air and chew on it to get it down into my lungs. I counted in my head. One...I was tired, so very Three...no song to play Six...sometimes the tormenter is the lover Nine...a nerve ending to nature's order Twelve...there is no karmic balance in the world Fifteen...God and science are one and the same Eighteen...I did not want to shoot anybody, not myself, not Maggie, not God. Yet I turned and pulled the trigger. In place of lead came the restless, dissonant voicing of the tritone. In my hands was the holy instrument. On the neck: my fingers, all of them intact at the quick, arranged in the death chord.

*Diabolus in musica*, the strum loud as God's laugh bent the weeds to the ground. It was my old guitar. It was my finger, and I could feel it. The crows flew to God, lined his outstretched arms in frontline infantry. The silo fell. The dogs of Van Buren

County, each and every one of us, howled. The tone bled until the echo shattered miles after it, leveling Michigan. When it was over my finger and the guitar were gone. In the dirt of the old plain laid Hal's smoking gun. I ran the forty paces to God and fell at his feet. The crows held fast. A lone hole in God's chest bled a single red line down his shirt, his pants, and into the ground. His own weapon was gone.

He said: "Sometimes the lover is the tormentor in order to be the lover renewed. I am not your obstructionist. I am your projectionist. I am the God, but there is a God of me, too."

The crows carried him off until they together blurred into one single violet raven against the bruised sheet of night. The arrows of stars evaporated into their longing targets, never meant for me. The knotty Midwestern mini-jungle rose again and closed in around me, and my nose emptied of the brown of so much corked smoke, toasted hostility, and Squamata waste. The desert a circle no more.

I wept. Phlegm choked out of my throat. I wailed for the guitar, I wailed for my finger, and I wailed for God. GOD I LOVE YOU. GOD I DON'T. GOD I SEE. GOD WHEN IN SONG. GOD WHEN A MISCREANT. GOD DON'T LAY DOWN WITH YOUR BROTHER'S WIFE. GOD CHECK YOUR SPERM. GOD STRETCH YOUR FINGERS. GOD TO BE A LEFTY. GOD HAVE YOU TUNNELED OUT OF CALIFORNIA. GOD SMELL THE BADLANDS. GOD IS THE NIGHT SO MUCH LONGER THAN THE DAY. GOD = TEARS + SLEEP. GOD SELFLESSNESS IS SELFISHNESS. GOD CANCEL THE SHOW. GOD HERE IS MY WIFE. GOD HERE IS MY BROTHER. GOD HERE IS MY CHILD. GOD HERE IS MY MOTHER. GOD HERE IS MY FATHER. GOD HERE IS MY FINGER. The eclipse of some hag moon hung like white shrapnel in the sky. Desperate like justice.

I could hear the scream of the waterfowl three thousand miles in the distance. The bear was downtown.

# Afterclap

I did not want to die in Michigan. Back in the house I wrapped Maggie. I scrubbed the walls, erasing the evidence, the final touches of putting the beholden to rest. After the walls I stripped the bed. When I moved to clean the floor I found the pruned clot. Next to it, the letter, opened, faceup. I read it:

*Dear Magg,*

> *I hope this finds you well, in good spirits. What good are words? Do they have music? The road, as I'm sure you've found, is long, and it's a shame that we, that I, tried to trick it into being so short. I'm writing to you, finally, because I've reached the wrong end of the rainbow. I've spent my days without life, or so I had convinced myself, and now the truth is falling like so much rain. Strange how in this dim hour the only vision I can conjure is of us shooting the eyes out of that damn ugly clown painting we won at the county fair. Oh, Maggie, how "sorry" is a contempt-*

*ible word. What does it sing? I spent these decades mostly silent but for this herald. I've told him about the clown, the life we had, and the life we wanted. And the life we lost. I just want you to know that despite miles and years and madness, some things do last forever.*

*All my love,*
*Best,*
*Hal*

*p.s. Don't hold onto this letter until it turns to dust. Don't torture yourself. Read it and know, that's all.*

They were his words. I was just the messenger.

When I finished inside the house I returned to the Hondo and burned the stained shrouds along with all of Hal's things I'd carried with me. Except for his rig. I burned the painting. I'd liked to have shot it up a little more. In a utility room inside the house I found a pickax and a shovel. The ground broke easily, warm and welcoming. I was a horse, and my sweat, full of toxins, full of time and full of hot balled night, trampled out of me and into the dirt. I buried Maggie out in the field. No marker. Just turned the soil. Simple, the countryside hopefully would still be the countryside. I loaded the grandfather clock into the Hondo. It was heavy enough that I ended up scraping it along the path from the house, and while trying to wrangle it into the car I cracked the glass and bent the long hand. To make it fit I had to put the passenger seat all the way back, lay the long case at an angle, and stick its head out of the rear driver's side window. Taking him home was almost more trouble than taking him out of The Amigo, but Hal in a way would finally be riding shotgun.

I left Gloria a short note that read:

*Dear Gloria,*

*I went to California to see about a bear.*

*Thank you for everything dear friend.*
*Love,*
*Maggie*

I drank the very last swallow left in the bottle of whiskey I'd given to Maggie. I wrote a short note to Hal and Maggie and Cyrus's would-be daughter, put it in the bottle, and sent it flying into the field out beyond the fallen silo. I got into the Hondo and headed for Indiana.

Passing through Bloomingdale, even though it wasn't noon yet, the Fourth of July festivities were well under way. For such a small town there was a big turnout, and it filled me with melancholy to imagine all of these warm-blooded creatures with all of their grave charms and wild ugliness—these fundamental alkali of the human disposition in the sordid order of things—alive with such heroically blind elation. The sound of firecrackers and sirens and patriots cheering, and the children of patriots. Death was at their doorstep. It was Independence Day.

Beyond Bloomingdale, I stopped at Great Bear Lake. I put the letter into Hal's cedar box, locked it, and tossed it to the fishes. A better angler than I ever could be, but no gunslinger to match my own in the sad but wanting nine-finger-dance, the thrush of his mouth finally ultimately holy and laid to rest.

There was still a third of whiskey left in my last fifth. I crossed the Indiana border and pulled over. Facing Michigan, I downed the wet gold, wondering how long I would last on my own. Lake Michigan rolled brilliant beneath the ascending sunlight, and except for the soft drum of ankle-slapper waves it was almost like facing the memory of Her Majesty, the Pacific Ocean. I reached into my pocket for Hal's finger bones. I put them to my lips, my nose. I listened to them. I rattled them around for a flash and then I threw them as hard as I could back over the state line. I left the empty whiskey bottle at the border. I got back in the car and headed a little south and mostly west.

I stopped to visit my parents just outside of Chicago. I even detoured for flowers. There was no more reason to race against The End alone. To step fast but softly into it, I decided, as gracefully and focused as possible and with all bills paid was the handle. Let it come, let it come. Let it come to me if it's the will. Let it catch me. Let it kick: It's never the end until it's the end. To fight something as truly godlike as Time was to court ruin, no matter the measurement of conceived loss, but I honestly wanted to live past the day.

At the grave I finally said goodbye to my mother and father. I sang a melody of songs for them, some mine, mostly not. While doing so, unconsciously, the fingers of my fret hand strummed the air along, the nub doing the best it could. I thought of Red. She had a really nice voice when she wasn't screaming, so the message in the bottle read.

Back on the road, I floored it for the Queen Califia. I had a promise to some elephant seals I had to make good on. Trying to outrun the arc of day, I sighted the Hondo; the car, the gun, the guitar indistinguishable. I prayed for the remaining fingers, mine and everyone else's. If the plug could wait just enough before being pulled, if God might lose just one hand against Time in the final throwdown, somewhere out along the highway I was bound to find another Guild M20 acoustic solid-top. Maybe in Des Moines, maybe Lincoln, Denver, Santa Fe. Maybe in the desert. Wherever it was time to stop for oil, I would look for it. I had some sins to confess to Bug Wallace. With a little luck and a lot of time, I might just figure a way to show that magnificent fat junkie son of a bitch some goddamn light. Who knows. What I know now is that no matter where I've been, where I've gone, and no matter how I've rolled those

165

bones, The Blues have run the game. I could hear them once more calling me home. Little Pam waiting at the bridge, her lips white looking for an answer. The ocean, the siren, with the ceaseless calling. And the Lord.

We can only live as long as the sun.

## CHORUS

*Time was time, and the time had come. And the world was silent for even a minute. And the silence was music. A knife slips from between ribs. Flesh does not eat its own. A page returns to a book. Sisyphus takes pause. The Queen of the Angels confesses. The dogs bury the bones. The crickets lay down their bows. The crows abandon the tree. Whose kiss melts oblivion?—A chord sounds: The geese fly into the sun. The elephant seals roll back. The bear takes the mount. Look: Agamemnon and Achilles at rest. The lone wolf arrested by God.*

# ACKNOWLEDGEMENTS

THE author and the musicians wish to thank: Advanced Audio, Akashic Books, Book Soup, Alexandra Infante Cornell, Drag City, Amy Ganser, Brian Gottlieb, James Greer, Hotel St. George Press, Hanna Hurme, Johanna Ingalls, Patrick Klem, Beth Lisick, Kurt Mangum, Alex Maslansky, Joe McGraw, Richard Medina, Narrow Books, Jeff Parker, Tamra Rolf, Scott Rothstein, and Jerry Stahl for helping us run the game.

To Aaron Petrovich, editor, clever devil, and all-around eyes of the hawk.

And to Tyson Cornell and Charles Day for tossing their teeth (and their money) into the fire. To Ben Flashman for similar reasons, illicit and legit.

And boundlessly to our gang, our loves, down on the E-Zee Street chicken farm and before and beyond: Elisa Ambrogio, Amy Hite, Eden Ruecker, Iris Ruecker, Becky Smith, and poor Jacky Boy—we might be propped scarecrows without you.

J OSEPH Mattson is the author of *Eat Hell* (Narrow Books), and his writing has appeared in *Ambit*, *Slipstream*, *Two Letters*, and more. An epical rambler—miles under him include work as a farmer, dishwasher, getaway driver, and in healthcare for the clinincally mentally insane— his home base is Los Angeles.

S IX Organs of Admittance tours multiple continents and has released over a dozen albums, including *Dark Noontide* (Holy Mountain), *School of the Flower* (Drag City), *Shelter from the Ash* (Drag City), and *Luminous Night* (Drag City), in addition to contributing the guns to even dozens more.

# EMPTY the SUN  Music by
# Six Organs of Admittance

1. Night to be Alone    2. Two Blades
3. Goodnight Hal    4. Twenty Paces
5. Clean the Wound    6. Lord, I have Returned
7. Blackened Road    8. Hacienda
9. Goddamn the Sun    10. Blacker Night
11. Still a Long Way    12. Piedras Blancas
13. Roll the Stone

O GODDAMN the SUN
Its LIGHT DIN'T Shine ON
Every ONE
O MAGGIE'S GONE
The Bottle's DONE
No Where to RuN.

Ben Chasny: Guitars, vocals, bells
Steve Ruecker: Guitars, pedal steel, vocals, rattlers, bowls

With:
Jack (RIP): Yelps on 2
Elisa Ambrogio: Vocals on 3, 7, 9
Becky Smith: Drums on 4, 5
Joseph Mattson: Elephant seal field recordings & echoplex on 12

Recorded in Deer Skull Hacienda (bulldozed) on E-Zee Street,
Encinitas, California, in August, 2008.
Mastered by Patrick Klem in Dunwoody, Georgia, in March, 2009,
www.klemflastic.com.